TO DWELL IN THE LAND

Elaine Watson

Serenade/Saga
BOOKS

of the Zondervan Publishing House
Grand Rapids, Michigan

TO DWELL IN THE LAND
Copyright © 1985 by The Zondervan Corporation
Grand Rapids, Michigan

Serenade/Saga is an imprint of Zondervan Publishing House,
1415 Lake Drive, S.E., Grand Rapids, Michigan 49506.

Library of Congress Cataloging in Publication Data

ISBN 0-310-46892-2

All Scripture quotations, unless otherwise noted, are taken from the
HOLY BIBLE: NEW INTERNATIONAL VERSION (North
American Edition). Copyright © 1973, 1978, 1984, by the Interna-
tional Bible Society. Used by permission of Zondervan Bible
Publishers.

Designed by Kim Koning

Printed in the United States of America

85 86 87 88 89 90 / 10 9 8 7 6 5 4 3 2 1

For Elsie and Will

My thanks to the people in the Archives Room in Frankfort, Kentucky, who directed me to the site of "Fort Liberty" and found for me personal letters from survivors of the destruction of the Fort.

CHAPTER 1

BERTIE LOOKED AT ANTON'S tall, slender body, stretched out along the stone wall behind her parents' farmhouse. He was leaning on one elbow, and he seemed to be peering past her into a distant place and time that were not a part of her world. She looked at his silky blond hair and his blue eyes, already framed with laugh lines in the corners.

"I'm glad you missed that ship," Bertie declared, startling his attention from his reverie. Her skirt ruffled in the breeze that came down from the blue-misted mountains above them to the west. "I'm glad we're starting for the wilderness lands next week, too. And most of all I'm glad you're going with us!"

Anton chuckled. "I'm not sure your Papa will be glad to have me along. I've got no proper identity papers any more."

"But they discharged you from that prison. Everybody knows that the Hessian soldiers captured at the Battle of Saratoga were finally allowed to go free. You're legally free to be here."

"I *was* legal," he said, "legal only if I got on the ship that was to take us all back to Germany. I thought I'd have plenty of time to come out here to look up some other folks who used to live near Frankfort. And then I found your family, and I guess I forgot about time."

Bertie took Anton's hands in hers. "Come over here with me," she said. She led him to her favorite spot, beneath a tree on whose friendly branches she had spent a good many childhood hours, dreaming and reading her mother's Bible and her own English grammar book. "Look," she said, with a wide sweep of her arm, "Papa says this rich farmland is like paradise.

"He told me once that when the pastor back home talked about Heaven he thought about America. But even so, we never expected all this beauty—and such freedom! Anton, tell me honestly, could you go back to the Old Country after seeing the Shenandoah Valley?"

Anton was not looking at the gently sloping fields and forests beneath them. He was looking at Bertie. "How your brown eyes sparkle when you get excited," he said.

"But you didn't answer my question." Her heart thumped in a peculiar way.

"If it was meant for me to miss that ship," Anton said, "I guess it was for some reason besides the sunshine on those fields. But I'd best be helping your father now," he said and then walked off toward the big barn.

Bertie began her own chore of raising a milk pail from the cool recess of the well and skimming cream from it. She knew Anton was helping her father sack what was left of last year's corn, and wheat, and oats. They would need seeds for planting after they had crossed the mountains and come into the fine farmland on the other side that awaited settlers. Especially settlers who were also smart German farmers. Peaceful peole who wanted no part of the Colonials' war.

Just as she was leaving the little milk house Bertie heard a sound that made her breath catch in her throat. From far down in the valley rose three mellow notes out of a horn that signaled to settlers for miles around the arrival of a pastor. When her father had returned from the village the night before, he told his family that a circuit-rider was coming their way. It was an opportunity they would not often have once they moved.

Bertie put her pail down and ran through a small flock of chickens, sending them angry and squawking across the grass. "Mama!" she called. "Did you hear the horn?"

Mrs. Meyer appeared at the door of their kitchen, wiping her hands on her apron. Her cheeks were flushed a deep red from work over a kettle in the fireplace.

"Thank the Lord!" she said. "I wouldn't like to start off for wilderness lands without a few prayers first."

Bertie had been saving her next question for some time and now she asked it in a hurry before she might lose her nerve. "Mama," she said, "with a pastor here, why don't we let him marry Anton and me before we start on our journey? Heaven only knows when we would have another chance to get married in the proper way."

"Has Anton spoken to you about marriage?" Mrs. Meyer asked, looking steadily at her daughter. "He has not spoken to Papa."

Bertie was silent. Anton had not said the words yet, but she was sure he would say them any day now.

Her mother nodded. "I thought so. And besides, you know why Papa can't let you marry Anton Marx."

"I realize he's only been with us a few weeks since he left that prison, Mama, but he's from Frankfort, too. It's not as though Anton were a real stranger. And if Papa is worried about his not having identity papers, I'm sure Anton can take care of that some time soon. Anyway, lots of people in the wilderness don't have identity papers."

"Not our kind of people, Bertie," her mother said. She reached out and smoothed her daughter's heavy dark hair back from her face.

Bertie pulled away slightly. "Then there's

something else, isn't there, Mama? I do believe sincerely Anton and I could make a good marriage."

"Yes, there are things Papa has not talked about with you. Anton's people back in Frankfort are not church people, Bertie. They are good farmers, it's true, but your papa wants more for his daughter. And there's something else. I understand Anton's father was killed when Anton was just a baby. Rumors about a violent way of life have traveled with them.

Bertie," she added, "Anton seems like a good fellow, but there's a glint of something secret in his eyes now and then. As though he's not the man he makes himself out to be. Papa's does not think he is the man for his daughter to marry."

"Oh, but Mama," Bertie began, "that's just foolishness! Anton's— "

"And now we'll say no more about it," Mrs. Meyer said as she turned and went back into the house.

CHAPTER 2

BERTIE SAT AMONG the women and children, waiting for the pastor to begin. It was just turning dusk in the valley, and starlight was already starting to pierce through a soft canopy of night above them. Because of the large crowd of Scotch-Irish and German farmers, as well as local traders and shopkeepers, the pastor had decided to hold services on the hillside rather than in the schoolhouse.

Bertie and her mother had spread their blanket next to a little grove of trees where the German men stood while smoking tobacco grown in their own tobacco patches and exchanging stories. The Scotch-Irish settlers and their families gathered in groups farther along on the hill.

Bertie ignored the women's conversations. She strained to hear what was going on under the trees. All the men were obviously eager to talk with her father, since he would be leaving the Valley soon, and with Anton, who still held an aura of mystery for them. Anton laughed and joked, and he told them tales about the Battle of Saratoga and about prison life, but beyond that, he said little about himself.

Old Herr Schultz, speaking in German, had not given up trying to get information out of him, though. "And with that green soldier's coat you still wear, faded though it is, Anton Marx," he said, "and those yellow pants, I guess you must be one of those Jaegers, those famous riflemen from Hess. Ya? Is that not so, Herr Marx?"

Anton laughed and answered him in English. "You like green uniforms. Mr. Schultz? How do you know a soldier doesn't sometimes steal a green uniform from a dead Jaeger? In war time a lot of things can happen."

Bertie saw her father look toward Anton. Mr. Meyer seemed to start to speak, but then he turned away. Why, Bertie wondered, didn't Anton just tell people what they wanted to know about him. She—and her parents—knew he had been a Jaeger, and that he had enough money, issued to him for his wartime services, to buy a horse and to finance his way into the wilderness. And then enough even to buy a farm.

Now Herr Schultz started to heckle her father. "Well, Herr Meyer," he said, "if you want to take an *honest* rifleman along with you to protect that pretty daughter of yours from Indians, maybe you're going to have to look some place else."

Bertie's father laughed, but not in his usual hearty way. "Any rifleman is welcome when people go into Indian lands, but I'm sure there will be plenty in our party."

Then August Herter, who owned a good farm with fine limestone buildings spoke, seriously. "Why *do* you intend to risk the lives of your wife and your daughter, George?"

Bertie's father pulled at his pipe for a moment. "Now days there are a good many other Germans going into Kentucke, August. The newspapers say there are 'floods' of them. We won't be alone. And even though the agreement with the Indian chiefs in '75 didn't work out, I believe what Col. George Rogers Clark did last year to open up the land for settlers was just what we needed. I think 1779 is a good year to make such a move."

"Many's the time you've told me this valley seems like paradise, George," Mr. Herter persisted. "So then how can a man give up paradise?"

Several of the men chuckled and waited for an answer. Bertie's father sighed and then in a low voice he spoke. "I came to his new land with my wife and baby to get away from some of what it seemed to me were evils around me back in the Old Country. Wars. Wars over religion and over property. Inheritances getting smaller and smaller when families tried to divide up that property. Princes deciding for us what we should do with our lives. Conscription of young men to fight those wars." He glanced briefly toward Anton.

Then he continued more loudly. "And it has been good here. Our German neighbors have made it all seem like the best of our life in the Old Country. We own a fine farm with a good farmhouse and sturdy barns. It is a sad thing for me to have to sell it now. A young family from Pennsylvania will live here when we leave."

This was news to Bertie. Would a child from the Pennsylvania family sit on a limb in her favorite tree? Excitement about their journey paled for a moment when she thought about another person using her bedroom — and her bed. Her new bed in Kentucke might well be only a platform hung from a wall in a log cabin. She had never lived in a log cabin. But her father was still talking. She moved over to the edge of the blanket.

"And now the war with Great Britain is coming closer to us. It looks as though we will have to take sides, even in this out-of-the-way place. I do not want to take sides. There is already talk of conscription these days, too. Would I fight for King George? I feel no ties with him and no allegiance to him. Or would I fight with those Americans here in the Colonies who rebel against what they say are unlawful taxes? I don't know. All I want to do is to be a good farmer. And I know there is rich farmland in the wilderness, where a lot of Germans are already settling."

When he stopped, no one said anything for a moment. Then Herr Schultz spoke up, loudly, "And what words do you have for us now, Anton Marx? Is that the reason you're going along to the Wilderness, too? To get away from soldiers? You, Anton, in that Jaeger uniform? And with that new Pennsylvania rifle?"

In the dusk Bertie could just make out Anton's sudden grin. "I'll find other uses for my rifle now," he said.

An uncomfortable murmur that started to rise from one side of the crowd stopped abruptly when the minister began to speak. While Bertie had been watching the men, someone had placed a small table at the edge of the crowd and set a candelabrum on it. The flickering light cast strange shadows over the lined face of the pastor. His black suit coat and trousers blended into shadows, but his white beard and his white hair, that fell to his shoulders from beneath his black hat, shone in the pale breeze-changing glow. He spoke in German.

"I have a treat for you tonight, my brothers and sisters," he began. "I have with me a young elder of the Presbyterian persuasion, who will preach in English. Then, when Rev. Burns is finished, I will address you in German. My education began in a Lutheran seminary in Berlin, but I have since been confirmed and ordained in the church of the Moravian brethren. These, my dear friends, are our credentials. And tonight we all gather together as Christians."

Bertie noted the handsome red face of the young Presbyterian minister, and she was even able to concentrate for a few minutes on his instruction. But Anton's presence only ten feet away in the darkness and the tone of mockery in his words to Herr Schultz at first floated through her mind, and then engulfed it.

Who *was* Anton Marx?

CHAPTER 3

Noises of night merged together outside the blockhouse. Horses snorting and neighing, cows lowing softly, an owl hooting in a nearby tree, wolves calling to one another in the mountains, laughter of men around a campfire near the river.

Bertie and her mother had retired inside the blockhouse with other women and their children. They were waiting for a large group to gather before they began their journey. Mrs. Meyer and Bertie shared a bed with a grandmother who had started her journey in Pennsylvania. Her daughter and three small children slept in an adjoining bed. One of the children coughed constantly, and the old lady snored.

"Oh, how I wish we could sleep on our own soft feather beds," Bertie whispered to her mother. Here they had been on their way only a week, Bertie thought, and already she sorely missed comforts she had always known.

"Try not to complain," her mother said in a low voice. "Papa will put out fether beds on the horses tomorrow." Then she added, "We are traveling in great comfort compared to our trip here from Germany. Because you were just a baby then, you can't remember the sickness and troubles we endured on our way to America. Those times were worse, my child. Now in a few more days we will settle down again, and Papa and Anton will plow some fields and build a house. A cabin at first, maybe. And you and I will plant a garden and an orchard. And then help the men plant corn and wheat, too, and herbs for our medicines. They tell me a person hardly needs to plow that rich limestone land in Kentucke. Crops spring right out of the ground, among the cane."

Bertie listened to her mother with only half her attention. She remembered the horror stories she had heard from others traveling with them about Indian raids, and shivered. Only the memory of her last meeting with Anton helped calm her.

She had been with him by the river, while Anton had picked up a few stones and made them skip across the surface of the wide, shallow river. He had stored his Hessian uniform in one of his saddle bags, and he wore a brown woolen jacket and pants he bought the day after the pastor's visit.

"Anton," she finally said, in that conversation that seemed so long ago, "Papa told us Col. Clark had cleared the Indians out of the place we're going to in Kentucke. That's not true, is it?"

Before he answered Anton sent another stone skipping across the water. Then he sat down on a flat rock and pulled Bertie down beside him. He put his arm around her. She felt safer, somehow, although she knew it was for only a moment.

"The Indians have rights, too, you know," he began. "I've read a lot, especially in French books and phamplets, about the way they live. We're robbing them of their hunting grounds and their sacred places. It's as though some brutal foreigners forced their way into the Cathedral at Cologne and destroyed it, and then lived on the ruins and kept us out. They fight back the only way they know how."

Bertie's father and mother had told her similar things about the Indians when she was a child, but all the Indians she had seen over the years had been friendly, or at least not hostile. And now that her parents were making this great move, she had assumed they knew it would be a safe one.

"But why do Indians do such terrible things to white people? Why don't they agree to treaties?"

Anton smiled sadly. "They've made treaties with us, and more often than not we've broken them. Whatever nastiness we get from them, we

have it coming, I'm afraid. But I hope you and I
— and your Mama and Papa — won't have to
suffer any of that nastiness. We'll try to outsmart
the Indians, if we can.''

He rose and looked up at the mountains above
them. ''And, come to think of it, white men don't
treat each other too well either, Bertie. Especially in war. Believe me, I could tell you stories a
lot livelier than any ones you have heard.''

Fully awake with the memory, Bertie turned
carefully in the bed so she would not disturb the
old lady or her mother. She thought of Anton's
arm around her, and once more — just for a
moment — she felt safe. *I might not feel safe
again for a long, long time,* she thought.

The next morning's misty sunlight revived
Bertie's spirits a little. When she left the blockhouse she found that during the night a half
dozen or more groups had come by various
routes to this central meeting place on the
Holston River. The air smelled of horses and
cows, and some slaves were at work clearing the
livestock area. Scouts on horseback, who had
made the trip to Logan's Fort in Kentucke many
times, were giving advice to men loading their
horses. Besides sacks of grain and clothing, there
were feather beds, spinning wheels, tools, cooking pots, even a cradle. Her father was loading
up their four horses, having sold their wagon.

*If scouts can come and go in Indian lands the
way these men seem to be able to do, maybe I*

21

shouldn't be so fearful, Bertie thought. She decided to put the terrible stories she had heard into the back of her mind, and fill it instead with prayers and thoughts of Anton. She loved him with a love that she knew no one could deny her.

"Good morning! And did you sleep well?" Bertie turned to find Rev. Burns standing next to her. The day after his sermon in the Shenandoah Valley the young Scot had decided to join the Meyers' party. He would begin a circuit in Kentucke, he said. And he would build a church there, too, as soon as he could.

Bertie smiled at him and nodded. He was a handsome, vigorous man, and really quite cheerful, she thought, in spite of his gloomy, religious beliefs. "Are your horses ready?" she asked.

"My horse, Mistress Meyer," he chuckled. "You are aware of the fact that I can hardly afford one horse. But I have my cooking pot and a change of linen. And, of course, my musket. I will have to hunt for game to put into my cooking pot."

"Didn't you bring bacon and cornmeal and dried pumpkin? If you don't have any of those, I'm sure we can share with you," she said. "And salt. You must have salt and herbs."

"That's kind of you, Mistress. The circuit pastor always has to exchange his services for food and shelter." He smiled down at her. "So it might be a marriage ceremony you'll want performed in your family before long," he said.

Bertie felt her cheeks grow warm. Rev Burns was, after all, a stranger, she thought, and he should not presume. He should know German women had good manners, though, so she replied, "Things like that are for parents to decide, sir."

He laughed, a loud and hearty laugh. "And for only parents to talk about, too!" he said. He walked off, shaking his head and murmuring, "These Dutch! They're all alike!"

Then Bertie saw Anton standing next to his handsome black horse only a short way across the clearing. He was grooming the horse's coat.

"Good morning, Anton," she said. "Will you have breakfast with us? Mama is frying some scrapple over near the blockhouse."

"Just give me a minute to finish this job," he said. What did that preacher want of you, Bertie? You must have told him a good joke to make him laugh that way."

"I didn't mean to," Bertie said. "Why do people call us 'Dutch,' Anton? There aren't many Dutchmen in America outside of New York City. At least that's what my schoolmaster said."

"Just plain laziness, Bertie. Or ignorance. We came from Deutschland, and Colonials can't pronounce that word very well, so they call us Dutch. That's my theory."

His voice rose a little. "And that preacher's pretty lazy in other ways, too. If he doesn't know enough to buy for himself a good Pennsylvania long rifle to use where he's going, he could be in for trouble. He'll probably expect the Lord — and people like us — to protect him. Well, the only one I'm going to protect will be Anton Marx!'' He looked down at her, and then he smiled. ''And you, Bertie. I won't let any bear or any Indian hurt you.''

Bertie hummed a little as she left Anton and hopped carefully from one relatively clean spot to another on her way back to her mother.

Why had Anton been so critical and angry when he talked about Rev. Burns? Because he was jealous! No matter what might happen during the hard journey ahead, she now felt sure of Anton's affection for her.

But, she decided, she would have to speak to Anton about his irreverant way of talking. His words sometimes made him sound almost ruthless. And proud.

Maybe that was one of the reasons her father did not want Anton to marry her.

CHAPTER 4

BERTIE PULLED HER HEAVY wool shawl up over her head. Mild air in the Valley had given way to sharp mountain wind. Now that she was riding into the lovely blue mist that had often hovered over peaks to the west of their farm, she found the mountainside only chilly and damp. More than once her horse stumbled on the slippery path. She held his reins tight to give him — and herself — confidence when he snorted in anger over having to pick his way on a route along a sheer cliff that dropped straight into a chasm below them.

Now Bertie could see why her father had left his wagon behind. Some settlers apparently did get small wagons through the Cumberland Gap, but broken wheels and discarded wiffle trees, along with bones of horses and cattle reminded travelers of the danger that still lurked beyond each new turn in the trail. Old tree stumps and fallen rocks helped to make the path treacherous, even for horses.

Bertie's mother rode ahead of her, only two horses behind their guide, and after Bertie came her father. Their mare followed. All of the horses were loaded with household goods and grain and tools. Bertie sometimes could see Anton at the end of the line of seventeen horses, nursing their slow cows over the rocks. He would still be on the trail below her while she climbed even higher into the mist. How his hair and his fine blond beard shone in patches of sunlight! Bertie wished she could ride beside him.

Two Scotch-Irish hunters rode just behind the mare. Early in the day Bertie had laughed at their songs and jokes. But now she was weary, and she tried to close her ears to their repeated rendition accompanied by swigs from a jug. Yet they sang on, endlessly.

In Cumberland Gap the cattle all died.

The men all swore and the women all cried!

For a while in the midafternoon she tried to make her conscious mind become blank, to close out the whole frightening world around her. Then she tried a prayer. But her tired brain responded only with a childish prayer, and it did not seem to do much good.

If Bertie could have turned her horse around, she would gladly have fled back to the warm, safe Shenandoah Valley.

The group had stopped only a few times to rest their horses. Now the sun was dropping behind the mountains, and Bertie felt utterly exhausted.

Then Peter Harris, their guide, called out, "Fort ahead! We'll spend the night here!"

While the men began to care for the horses and cattle, Bertie and her mother and the three other women in their party slid off their saddles, their joints stiff, and walked together over to the fort. The guide told them there would be glowing sticks inside that they could use to start their cooking fires. A gray-bearded old man who was selling harness parts and bullets, among other things, said to Mrs. Meyer, "You're going to need water bags, ma'am. I've some some fine, clean innards of elk to sell. After you cross the Powell River tomorrow there ain't going to be any water for a good long time. You and those horses of yours could get mighty thirsty."

Peter Harris had come inside with the women. He grinned at the old man and said," Henry, don't try any of your tricks on this bunch. These ladies are too smart for the likes of you!"

Harris turned to Bertie's mother. "In the summer, ma'am, it does get pretty dry up here, but now in March we'll be lucky if we don't drown under some of the waterfalls coming down out of the mountains."

"Do horses ever slip on wet rocks, Mr. Harris?" Bertie asked.

He chuckled. "Yep, Mistress, they sure do.

Many's the horse I've had to shoot after he took a bad fall." He paused for a moment and looked down at her. "But I never shoot the rider," he whispered.

Then he laughed again and went over to warm his hands by the fireplace. "You ladies can do your cooking in here," he said. "There's only a small charge, and it won't add much to your bill."

"Thank you," Mrs. Meyer said. Another group of six chattering women had already begun to put a big kettle of water on the fire. "But I believe our family will eat together out-of-doors tonight."

Harris pulled a glowing stick from the fire and handed it to her mother. Then he took one himself and went outside.

It was becoming crowded in the dark, smoky room. Old Henry suddenly appeared at Bertie's side. "I got something else to sell, Mistress," he said. "Something you're going to need." He took a small tin box out of his pack. "This here is snake root. You've never in your life seen snakes like the rattlers on the Cumberland Trail." He grinned at her. His one dark tooth gleamed faintly in the firelight. "And them snakes will hit your leg no matter how high you carry it. Or the critters'll get to your horse's belly."

Bertie turned and ran after the other women. She heard Henry chortling behind her.

On her way across the clearing she noticed

Rev. Burns and Peter Harris starting a fire together.

After they had eaten their stew made of dried vegetables and dried meat, Anton said, "I believe I'll walk down toward the river. I'm told we'll have to cross it early tomorrow."

"You should have company, son," Mr. Meyer said. "I'll walk along."

"I'll come, too, Papa," Bertie said. "I need a walk after sitting on a horse all day."

Her father seemed about to say no, but her mother said, "You do that, child. There's not enough work to keep you here."

Bertie walked between her father and Anton. The sun had now long disappeared behind the mountains, and a misty dusk was beginning to settle in. The long spring evening would last another hour, though.

"Do Shawnee Indians still live in these forests?" she asked. "Aren't we on one of their trails? I saw strange markings on some of the trees today."

Mr. Meyer glanced at Anton. Anton was carrying his rifle. "Our guide insists there's no danger," Bertie's father said. "He told me the Shawnee and the Cherokee are fighting each other west of here nowdays."

Bertie still listened, however, for the crack of a twig in the forest around them, knowing of course, that no Indian would let anyone hear him if he did not want him to.

Within a few minutes they reached the river. Spring rains and run-offs had swelled it and quickened its currents. But their horses would certainly be able to cross it. It was clear that every day travelers crossed here, just beyond the fort.

They sat to rest for a moment on a log near the river. The trees were alive with evening bird songs. Upstream three deer drifted down to the water's edge to drink.

"Just beyond the river is the place Daniel Boone buried his son after the Shawnee tortured and killed him," Anton said. "But that was back in 1773. He buried the boy's body up on the mountainside. I understand the pile of stones that marks the grave is still there."

"Peter Harris told me Boone visits the grave every time he's in this area, to see that the stones are still in place," Mr. Meyer said. "Peter's been up there himself. I would have ridden up there, too, if we had stopped for the night a little earlier. People who use this trail owe a lot to Daniel Boone."

Suddenly Bertie remembered Henry's warning about snakes. "I wonder if rattle snakes do strike at travelers on the trail," she said.

Mr. Meyer and Anton looked at each other, and then they both burst into laughter. "So old Henry got to you, too," Anton said. "He made the rounds, I guess. And he even sold three tins of rattle snake root. He must have quite a business."

"It's too early for snakes up here, Bertie," her father said. "Worry about mud slides, if you have to worry about something, but not about snakes."

"Well, then, I'm not even going to worry about mud slides, either. We will surely have a good, safe journey!" Bertie said. She put tomorrow's frightening, exhausting ride out of her thoughts. And she was delighted to see Anton and her father laughing together.

But when they made their way back up to the fort, Bertie still listened tensely for the crack of a twig beneath a moccasined foot somewhere out in the darkness.

CHAPTER 5

BERTIE IDLY WATCHED groups of settlers going about their work in the clearing outside Logan's Fort, near the end of the Wilderness Road. Her family would leave the road here.

The spring sun in Kentucke County felt different from sunshine she had known before. Here in this rich, rolling country, afternoon heat already warmed the trampled earth. "And what will the sun be like in August?" she wondered. She recalled stories Anton had told her about Hessian soldiers fighting in battles along the Colonials' eastern coast. They had been unaccustomed to such hot summers, and a good many of them collapsed from heatstroke.

But nights were still cold. It was hard to get used to this countryside. She hoped she would feel at home after they finally reached the acreage her father had bought. Since Kentucke was a county in Virginia, Mr. Meyer had made his purchase at a local government office before he left the Shenandoah Valley. He was enthusiastic about his new farm. Bertie decided not to annoy him with her feeling of uneasiness.

Their party of settlers and hunters had seen no hostile Indians anywhere along the trail. Apart from their sudden fears when a swollen river had washed Rev. Burns and his horse away, Bertie remembered only long, exhausting rides. Now and then, though, she had known a few moments of pleasure when they would come upon breathtaking views from the Cumberland Gap. She did mention her uneasiness to her mother, however, the day after they reached Logan's Fort.

"I know what you mean, Bertie," Mrs. Meyer had said. "I felt much the same way when we first got to America. A person has to learn to live with adjustments, my child. What your father wants," she paused briefly, and then went on in a firm voice, "and what *I* want, is the best for all of us. You must believe that. How else could we go on?"

Bertie thought about the way her mother had paused in mid-sentence, and the pause somehow comforted her. She was not alone in her uneasiness.

Since Anton was due back before long from his hunt for rabbits, Bertie was waiting for him outside the gate. Above her on three corners of the fort rose two-storey blockhouses. Although there had been no major Indian attacks since the one a couple of years earlier that almost destroyed the fort and all of its inhabitants, sentries still kept watch in the blockhouses. An apprehensiveness that never really left her these days quieted a little when she glanced up at the young guards in their squat, stockade-like towers.

Then Bertie saw Anton's black stallion raising dust and scattering chickens when he rode out of the forest onto the trampled dirt west of the fort. She ran to meet him, making her way past cows and pigs and their various owners, and two families who were packing a small wagon. For the first time she noticed that her father was in the crowd, buying pigs from a local settler.

Anton smiled down at her. Once more Bertie noted that his, friendly as it was, did not reach his eyes. More often than not lately his expression looked rather grim. He got off his horse and walked beside her back to the gate. "I'll take these rabbits to your mother," he said. "Hold Herod for me, Bertie. I want to walk him for a few minutes."

Bertie stroked Herod's sleek neck. "If Anton wanted to name you after a king in the Bible," she murmured, "I think he could have made a better choice."

When Anton returned she laughed and said, "Why didn't you give your horse a name like 'Solomon'? Or even 'Saul'? King Herod was not nice at all."

"But Herod is not such a nice horse," Anton said, again with that odd, grim smile. "And his owner's not such a nice man, either, Bertie."

She kept her eyes lowered, still stroking Herod's neck, to hide her confusion. All at once she felt a hard grip on her arm, just above her elbow.

"Come along with me, Bertie," Anton said, "while I walk Herod. There are things you and I have to talk about."

Bertie shook her arm free. His hand felt nothing like the hand of someone who loved her. She walked a little apart from him while they made their way across the clearing. to look back.

After a few moments he spoke. "We'll stop here." He tied Herod's bridle to a low branch. He sat on a stump of what had been a giant oak and pulled her down beside him.

"Bertie," he said, "I'm trying to do the right thing, believe me. You'll have to trust me when I say that. Do you trust me?"

She looked at him, at the face that became dearer to her night after night when it invaded her dreams. Finally she said, "Those are pretty strange words coming from a man I . . . well . . . from a man I believed might want to . . . . " She could not go on.

"To ask you to marry him?" Anton asked.

"Yes," she breathed.

Anton was quiet, too. Then he rose and began to walk, aiming hard, angry jabs at low branches with his rifle butt.

When he stopped he was standing above her. "Bertie," he said, "I can hardly keep away from you." He clenched the fist not holding his rifle. "I was brought up, though, to know the difference between honorable intentions and ones that are not so honorable."

"But you are a good man," she said. "A decent man. A soldier."

His smile was rueful. "Those things don't always go together," he said. "Being a soldier sometimes gives a man some rough edges. And then, too, Bertie, your father does not trust me."

She knew he spoke the truth. "Maybe there are things in your past he wonders about," she said. "Maybe you joke too much about such things."

"And maybe that's the only way I can face them."

Bertie knew she must not let this moment pass. "Can't you tell me, Anton?" A thought had been nagging at the edge of her mind. "Might it be that you have made a commitment — with someone else?"

Anton relaxed. Then he smiled. A real smile. He took her hands and pulled her up. For the first time he put his arms around her. "There *are* problems, my dear Bertie," he said. "But that is not one of them." He held her head against his chest, her cheek against the rough wool of his jacket. She could feel his heart beat. His jacket smelled faintly of woodsmoke and of horses.

Bertie put her arms around his waist, and she closed her mind to the future. With her eyes shut she felt submerged in the pleasure of Anton's strong, affectionate embrace.

When she opened her eyes she saw her father standing at the edge of the clearing. The expression on his face recalled for Bertie pictures from her childhood Bible stories, pictures of angry Old Testament prophets denouncing the children of Israel.

CHAPTER 6

BERTIE TOOK HER arms from around Anton's waist and pushed him away slightly, not looking back toward her father. She felt guilty. But why should she feel guilty?

Mr. Meyer's voice cut through the space betwen Anton and Bertie. "And what have we here?"

Anton sighed. Bertie hoped he would not try to make a joke, the way it seemed he so often did in order to deal with problems. Now that her feeling of guilt was passing, she began to feel angry. Angry with her father, with Anton, and with herself, too, for not standing up to both of them.

She turned toward her father. "I'm glad you're here, Papa," she said. "I have something to say to you. Anton has asked me to marry him." Mr. Meyer, his face still stormy, walked into the clearing. "I know you and Mama were afraid Anton might have an attachment somewhere else, Papa, and so you were not sure about his good intentions," she went on, words tumbling out rapidly. "But that's not the way it is, Papa. Anton is free to marry, and he has made his affections known to me."

Mr. Meyer's face relaxed slightly. "That appears to be obvious," he said.

Still Anton said nothing. Unuttered words hung heavy in the air.

Finally Mr. Meyer broke the silence. "Well, Anton? And what have you to say for yourself?"

Anton's familiar grim, sad look had returned. "It's true, Mr. Meyer," he said. "I would like to marry Bertie."

Bertie's father turned to her. "And you, child?" he asked. "Do you understand what this man is asking of you?"

"Of course, Papa. You must not make it so hard for us. I'm convinced we can have a good marriage. We have had the same kind of training in our homes and the same kind of religious teaching, too. And we have love for each other. Isn't that the way it was with you and Mama? I think Mama would give her consent if you were not so prejudiced against Anton, Papa."

"Then tell her, Anton," Mr. Meyer said. "Tell her what you have told me."

Anton cleared his throat. "It's true, Bertie, that your father and I have discussed some of

39

these things. I'm afraid my home life was not like yours. I was reared in the home of a forester, not the home of a farmer."

"But what difference could such a thing make?" Bertie cried. "Your family comes from Frankfort, too, just the way ours does. When we were children we saw the same hills. And the same sunrises."

"Tell her more," said Mr. Meyer.

"There are other problems, Bertie. Some of them I have not discussed with your father. And I cannot discuss them with him — or with you. Because they are still too deep inside me.

"But there is something we have talked about. There is the matter of my having no papers. No identity. In Virginia, even here in Kentucke County, a man who fought as a Hessian soldier for the Royalists is often among friends. But when the fighting is over, where will his friends be? Citizens of this county will probably side with the winners, whoever the winners are. But I, with no papers, would be an outsider, outside the law. And so would my family."

"But you can go back to Germany and set all of that straight, Anton," Bertie said.

"Not until the conflict is over. I do not want to go back into the Jaegers. I was conscripted, and as a youth I followed directions. Even though I was trained to be a soldier, I do not want to fight again."

"So you see, Bertie, there are problems," her

father said. "Mama and I would like you to wait."

Bertie felt great relief. "Of course we can wait," she said. "We'll wait, Anton. Won't we?"

Anton looked at her. There was little tenderness in his eyes. "No, Bertie," he said. "I cannot wait. I have told your father this. I'm not sure how long I can trust myself to hold to those honorable intentions I spoke about a few minutes ago."

He turned to her father. "I intend to leave your family, Mr. Meyer," he said, "and to strike out on my own, if your daughter and I cannot marry now."

"But Papa needs you, Anton," Bertie said. "He's counting on you!"

"There are other young men who might throw in their lot with us," her father said. "Rev. Burns is looking for a place to settle and to build a church. I would be pleased to assist him in his plans. He would not have the forest wisdom or the farming ability this young man has, but he would be willing to learn, I'm sure."

Bertie was appalled. Again words spilled out, words she would never before have used with her father. "Isn't it enough that you took me away from a safe home and brought me to this frightful place, Papa? And now you want to take away the man I have grown to love, too? And to replace him with that Scot!" She paused. She must be fair. "Of course Rev. Burns is a fine man, too, Papa, but not the one for me."

"I was not trying to make a match for you, Bertha," her father said. "I have other concerns that have nothing to do with a marriage for my daughter."

The sun had dropped behind the trees. Bertie shivered a little and drew her shawl more tightly around her. Her mind raced. Could she persuade her parents that this marriage should take place? Probably not. There was only one thing to do.

"Papa," she said, "then if Anton will have me, I'll go with him. Rev. Burns can marry us before we leave."

Her father stared down at her in disbelief. Then he turned to Anton.

"And what do you, a responsible Christian, say to such a statement a man must hear from his daughter?" he asked.

Anton smiled down at Bertie. A real, affectionate smile. "I'd say, sir, that I'd have to agree with your daughter. We'll get married, and then, if you will allow us to, we'll both help you settle your homestead here in Kentucke County."

Mr. Meyer looked for a long moment at the two of them, now standing with an arm around each other.

"So be it," he said. "But remember, my child, I have opposed this union."

CHAPTER 7

BERTIE AND ANTON sat together on a log and
watched a warm October sun beginning to slip
behind a hill on the other side of the valley.
Below them they could see Bertie's father bring-
ing a pail of milk into the cabin where her mother
was resting on a stool just outside the door,
knitting. Even at the end of a day of hard work,
her mother sat straight-backed.

The heavy fragrance of late summer weeds and
the calls of birds in the forest around them
created for Bertie a kind of brief, enchanted
moment, just before the early autumn dusk
would settle in. Chances for her and her husband
to enjoy the beauty of the nature around them
alone were scarce and she relished every moment.

"It looks like a fairyland down there," Bertie

said. "Our little cabin and barn and our cleared fields remind me of pictures an artist drew to illustrate old German myths I read in school." She laughed. "Papa could be a gnome, rising out of the shadows on the other side of our barn, where our cows, like mean Nibelings, hoard our gold, our milk. Papa rescues it for us!"

"Your father? A gnome, Bertie?" Anton laughed, too. "I think he'd prefer to be Siegfried, rescuing gold from those evil Nibeling cows. Cows that wander away in the forest, or eat weeds that make them sick so we can't use their milk for our cheese." He laughed again. "Evil, black-hearted cows."

Bertie looked at Anton with curiosity. He had shared her family's summer of hard work and their fine harvest. He was one of them. Almost.

But he still seldom talked about himself. They all knew by now that he'd had a good education, a much better one than any of the rest of them — for all their concern with schooling and with proper use of the English language.

"Do you see a fairyland when you look down the hillside?" she asked. "Did you read about such things, Anton, when you were a little boy in Hesse?"

"Of course. But I was required to learn Greek and Latin in school, too," he said, "and I guess I liked Greek myths best of all. With the dying of summer I think of the journey Persephone must soon make to the underworld. And while she is gone, the earth will die, too, for a little while. And when I hear these birds in the forest around us, I think of the golden songs Orpheus sang. Songs that were so beautiful he charmed the god of the underworld in order to rescue his loved one, Euridice.''

Such stories were new to Bertie, and she was eager to hear more about the doings of these strange, ancient god-like people. But just now she was content to be lulled by the magic of Anton's voice. He spoke in a lilting baritone, with a hint of laughter always just below the surface.

"We have a fine composer of operas these days, a German named Chrisophe von Gluck," Anton went on. "He goes back to Greek myths for stories in his operas in a way I find exciting. When I was a boy I had a chance to attend a performance of his 'Orfeo ed Euridice' in Vienna. I have never quite gotten over that experience.''

They were both quiet for a few moments. Very soon they would have to go back to the cabin.

"Anton," Bertie said, "when I'm here with you like this, just for a little while I'm not sorry I had to leave the Shenandoah Valley. But I think the fine house I grew up in will always seem like home to me. Don't you feel like that about one particular place you've lived?''

Anton took a deep breath. "Bertie," he paused for a moment and then went on. There is much I cannot tell you yet. My father died in battle. And that, coming as it did when I was so young, made me despise the military training that was required of me as a forester's son. Then I was conscripted by the Duke to fight for his cousin the British King—here in America. Being conscripted caused me problems I'm not sure I will ever be able to deal with."

Anton stared into the gathering dusk. "Just give me a little more time," he said. "I'll work it all out in my mind. Being with you, and with your father and mother gives me the most peace I have known for some time, but the war here is making me question so many things. From the first I have had little regard for this revolution against a lawful monarchy. But I know now I have even less regard for the right of monarchs to treat their subjects in abominable ways. I guess some of the ideas those Athenians had about democracy moved me as much as their myths did."

He paused, and Bertie could just make out the shadow of Anton's hand as he passed it over his face.

Then he went on. "And I've learned, Bertie, that princes and generals, people I was taught to respect and never to question are not always decent, honest men. In time of war, especially, men — and women, too — often turn into animals. Worse than animals."

In the darkness Bertie felt Anton's arm around

her waist. He stood and lifted her to her feet. "Just now I'm content to be here with you on a farm in Kentucke County, Virginia. The Indians have been quiet and our harvest has been good. What more can we ask?"

Bertie hugged him even tighter to her, and they started down the hill with their arms still around each other. "Anton," Bertie said, "you learned so much more in school than I did. But did you study your catechism, too?"

Anton's laugh was abrupt this time, and a little mocking. "I did tell you my father died when I was still a small boy. Well, he was killed in a war over religious beliefs. As a child, Bertie, I read the catechism my father wanted me to, and then after he was gone, the kind my mother believed. Yes I have studied catechism."

Bertie had to ask the next question, even though it seemed impertinent.

"And those gods and goddesses you are so fond of, Anton. Are they as real to you as the people in the Bible?"

His arm tightened around her again. They were at the cabin now. He turned to face her, and then he held her head close against his shoulder. "Nothing is real for me, Bertie, but you," he said. "You are my whole world." He paused. "I know that's not what you really want to hear, if you fear for my soul's health, but that's the way it is."

CHAPTER 8

"THIS IS A CHRISTMAS day we can tell our grandchildren about."

Bertie's father was sitting on a three-legged stool at the end of the table, smoking his pipe. Around the table, on a wooden chest and on a bench made from board over two buckets, sat Bertie and Anton and Rev. Burns. Bertie's mother had moved from the table to a stool next to the fireplace. Her fingers moved tirelessly over her knitting. Their coffee, concocted from a mixture of local grains, tasted rather bitter, but drinking a second cup of it in a leisurely way after they had eaten their traditional cake filled with dried fruits, somehow evoked for them happier Christmas days in years now long past.

"It's a pleasant thing for us to have a pastor here in our family to help us celebrate a holy day," Bertie's father went on. "Even if," he added with a chuckle, "the pastor doesn't really believe in our family's way of enjoying Christmas Day."

Rev. Burns smiled. "In the Old Country people made too much of Christmas," he said. "The way they behaved was scandalous, and it was often hardly a celebration of a holy day. The English ate like pigs, and the Irish drank themselves into a stupor. I suppose Germans were more circumspect," he glanced at his host, smiling again, "but then I had no way of judging German folk in those days."

Bertie's dinner of venison and beans had upset her stomach a little, as food so often did these days. The last few months had been difficult ones. Although her parents had come to accept Anton's presence there was always lurking nearby their deep disapproval of him for his shadowed past, of her for the way she had insisted on their quick marriage — with Rev. Burns called upon to officiate just before they all left the fort for the land her father had bought — and now, even of her pregnancy. The summer's hard work, an early winter, and her weakened condition had begun to take their toll on Bertie. She had to force herself to keep up an appearance of ordinary good nature.

"Why don't we all tell what our Christmases were like ten years ago?" she said. "I'll wager a Christmas day in Edinburgh was a lot different from one in Hesse, or from one in the Shenandoah Valley." She lingered over the sweet syllables in "Shenandoah."

Bertie looked about the dim, smoky room. In the firelight her loved ones' faces, in repose, all looked careworn and tired. In the shadowy corners of the room stood the spinning wheel and two chests filled with clothes and linens. From the walls hung kitchen tools. Fold-up beds were strapped to the walls for the day. A thick hemp rug covered the cold dirt floor. It was far different from the atmosphere Bertie now recalled from ten years before.

Then she realized that not one of the others had responded to her question.

"Well, I'll start," she said. "When I was a little girl I suppose I just felt happy about Christmas. I didn't have to worry over hunting for venison or turkeys or over having enough food for our cattle, or even over any household problems the way grown-ups did. When I was ten all the neighbors gathered in the schoolhouse, and we sang hymns and funny old songs in German. That year the school children put on a program, the way we always did. I recited a poem in English that Shakespeare wrote about what he called the seven ages of man, and my best friend, Katie, sang a beautiful lullaby." She paused. "I wonder if she is singing it to her little children this Christmas day." She shook from her mind the image of Katie, safe and warm—

and maybe lonely—back in the Shenandoah Valley.

"Next year," Anton said, "you can sing that lullaby to our little one. And we will all be together in the fine new house your father and I are already planning." Bertie leaned closer to Anton and put her arm through his. It would be good to have a large, comfortable house again.

Bertie's mother looked up from her knitting. "Ten years ago," she said, "I was grieving over the fact that I knew I would never be able to give Bertie a little brother or sister. And," she added, glancing toward her husband, "to give my husband a son to help him till the good land the Lord has always given us."

Only recently had Bertie begun to realize what the miscarriages her mother suffered must have cost her in grief and in health. Bertie had been a happy child, in a happy home, and now she knew much of that atmosphere of security and joy had been created by a mother who must often have felt anything but joyous.

"Ten years ago," her father said, "your mother and I came to a decision on Christmas day. We decided we would stay in Virginia and make our home a permanent one here among our friends from the Old Country. We talked about plans for the new barn I would build during the next year. There were rumors over on the Coast of problems with England, but I never thought it would come to war."

He moved his big body restlessly on the stool. He always seemed to be eager for more work, and for more and smarter ways to get a job done. Bertie now knew that part of the bitterness often creeping into his conversation these days resulted from his inability to manage his life the way he had planned to. For one thing, although Bertie knew her father loved her dearly, there had been no sons to help him farm. Then the war had come along, upsetting his life in a drastic way. And, finally, he felt his daughter had betrayed him when she scorned his advice about marriage.

Now he puffed his pipe with short, quick puffs and stared into the fire.

"Yes, Mr. Meyer," Rev. Burns said. "The war has upset all our lives. It was just ten years ago that I was making a decision that would change my life. As a schoolboy I was a terror. My poor widowed mother tried her best, but the rowdy lads at the shipyard and the good money they made looked much more inviting to me than those dull school books."

He laughed. "But if I hadn't been part way down that broad road that leads to destruction at one time myself, how could I understand today what tribulations other poor sinners are going through?"

"And you made your decision on Christmas day?" Bertie asked.

Rev. Burns got up and put another piece of

wood on the fire. The pine log crackled and snapped and sent out sparks. Then he stood for a moment with his back to the fireplace. "I went to church that day with my mother and our pastor read the gospel story about the shepherds. 'Good tidings to all people,' the angels told the shepherds. During that night 'good tidings to all people' kept ringing in my ears. And the next day I walked over to the pastor's home and told him I'd like to take those good tidings to people in heathen lands.

"Now," he went on, "I'm going to be able to build a church, here in Kentucke County. We Presbyterians don't seem to be as successful as the Moravians are in ministering to the savages, but there are a good many other souls who will need me."

Everyone was quiet for a moment. It was evident that all of them were waiting to hear how Anton Marx had spent Christmas Day ten years before.

But Anton got up and reached for his coat, where it was hanging on a peg near the door. "Savages?" he asked. "I think the use of the word 'savages' depends on a person's point of view, doesn't it, Rev. Burns?" Then he turned to Bertie's father. "I'll give you a Christmas gift, sir," he said. "You rest here by the fire this afternoon. I'll milk the cows and feed them, and take care of the horses and pigs, too."

When he went out, he closed the door softly behind him.

CHAPTER 9

BERTIE STOOD IN THE cabin door and waited for Anton's return from Fort Liberty. Every hour that Anton was away stretched far beyond the usual length of hours. His warmth, his gaity, his lean, handsome face and lithe body became dearer to her with every passing day.

Inside the cabin, working at a cooking pot over the fireplace, her mother was making a stew of venison and dried beans. Their bean barrel was running low. Dangerously low. They hoped Anton would be able to buy beans and salt for the household and oats for their horses. If the weather should finally break, there would soon be new grass for the horses and cows, but now the grass stored in their barn was nearly gone.

A late March sun was warm on Bertie's face. The sun was just beginning to melt great drifts of snow that still covered the north sides of hills. Soon, Mr. Meyer said, rivers would rise and valleys might flood. It was good to know that their safe homestead farm on sloping land above a valley floor saved them from such worries, but there were other more serious worries.

Shawnee Indians at trading posts told white settlers that this had been the worst winter anyone could recall. As bad as the prolonged misery of winter had been, though, other news the Shawnee brought was even more disheartening. Not news, really, but hints and threats that foretold immanent peril for farmers and trappers.

It was becoming evident that the war in the east was going badly for the British, but here in the west they still had power. And they had convinced Cherokee and Shawnee tribes that the white settlers were enemies who would soon overrun their hunting grounds and their sacred places. Indeed, white settlers were beginning to pour into Kentucke County again by the thousands, even as the long, hard winter was ending, and the Indians saw truth in stories the British told them. Now, it was rumored, British officers in the north were paying bounty for scalps and ransom money for settlers delivered alive to Detroit.

The day before, Bertie had heard her father and Anton talking in back of the cabin, where they were sawing logs in preparation for a new house, a house with a wooden floor and planed boards for walls. Mr. Meyer had told Anton about his ride earlier in the day on snowy Indian trails that led toward the Licking River. He said he'd wanted to check conditions along streams swollen with run-offs.

When he had seen no signs of life at the Nortons' cabin less than three miles away, he stopped to investigate. At the barn he'd found the cattle slaughtered, with the best meat stripped away. He had hesitated to enter the cabin, fearful of what he might discover. And, indeed, sprawled on the cabin floor he had found Mr. Norton, now at least several days dead. His scalp was gone. There was no sign of the man's wife nor his small son.

"They're probably well enough off," Anton said. "Living with a Shawnee tribe." He laughed. "Maybe the boy will grow up to attack us, too, some day. Or whoever survives us here."

"I don't always care for your idea of a joke, son," her father had said. "That was a sad hour for me. I will go back tomorrow to try to break through the frost and dig a grave."

"My jokes keep me going," Anton said. "It's always been that way. I'll ride along with you tomorrow. But we won't want to tell Bertie about this. She needs to keep good health in her mind as well as in her body these days."

Bertie now stood in the doorway remembering the men's conversation, closing her eyes to the bright sunlight. But she could not close off terrifying pictures in her mind of their neighbor in his cold, deserted cabin, and what his wife and his little boy might be enduring as captives among Indians. Indians who were growing increasingly angry and hostile.

Bertie sighed and went back to sweeping a hemp mat spread over the dirt floor. Now that ground around the cabin was thawing, their mats were always damp.

Then she sank onto a stool by the fireplace and took up her knitting. "Mama," she asked, "did you have pains long before I was born?"

"No," her mother said. "You were an easy child to carry. But then my life was easier in those days than your life is now. When a woman has worries, her baby knows it and becomes a little worried, too, Bertie. Try to calm your fears. Saying a few more prayers to myself after Papa finishes with Scripture reading at night helps me. Maybe that would help you, too." "I know I should not let myself think about what could happen to any of us, any day," Bertie said. "I heard Papa and Anton talking about the Nortons, Mama, and I'm really awfully frightened now. Probably my poor baby won't even get to see the light of day."

Mrs. Meyer looked at her daughter for a long minute. "It's harder for women than it is for men," she said. "Men can move about. We so often just have to sit and wait. But women have always done this waiting, my child. Remember all those stories of strong women in the Bible? And in other books you read in school? When their waiting is over, women have to act, too, and act wisely.''

She rose and stood beside Bertie, pushing the hair back from her daughter's forehead. ''Men have their own kinds of strength. But it's not the same as ours.'' ''I think we can understand theirs better than they can ever know how we think and feel.''

''Anton says if the Shawnee attack, he'll take me to the stockade at Fort Liberty. I'll be safe there.''

Her mother smiled. ''I'm glad you feel confidence in your husband,'' she said. ''But don't forget that he must count on your help, too. Anton needs you as much as you need him.''

Bertie stored her mother's words away. In her narrow world of nausea and pains, of the smoky room and the bitter cold, of increasing terror inside her mind and outside their cabin walls, it seemed to her that only the welcoming oasis of Fort Liberty kept her from losing hold completely.

CHAPTER 10

BERTIE WOKE TO THE distant sound of musket fire. *Musket fire!* Musket fire meant an Indian attack. She stretched her hand across the featherbed and found Anton's place empty, but still warm. Then she saw the figure of her husband framed in the doorway against a starry June sky. From the other pull-down bed she heard her father rustling out of the sheets and her mother's low cry on awakening. "Don't disturb Bertie," she whispered.

"I'm awake, Mama," Bertie whispered back. "How far away are the Indians?"

Then Anton helped her from the bed. "Get some clothes," he said. "I'm putting you and the featherbed on Herod. We'll be at Fort Liberty before sunrise."

Bertie groaned a little when her father lifted

her up to sit behind Anton. Part of the featherbed cushioned her, and the rest, where it was not securely strapped, billowed on either side of the horse. She could not reach around Anton's waist, so she clung to his jacket.

"You're sure you won't go with us?" Anton asked.

"This is my land, children," Mr. Meyer said. "I will rely on protection from Almighty God and from my long rifle."

"And you, Mama?" Bertie asked. "Aren't you afraid to stay? You could go along with us and live at the Fort for a few days. Wouldn't you like to see your grandchild?" Even as she asked it, she knew it was a cruel thing to do, to ask such a question.

Her mother reached up and put her hand on Bertie's arm. "I'll come to be with you as soon as I can," she said. "The child is not due to be born for another week. Perhaps you can even come back here before then. You have Anton, my dear. Your Papa needs me here."

"There will be women at the Fort to take care of Bertie," Anton told her parents. "Try not to worry."

Musket fire now seemed to be coming from some place just over the hill above them. Anton kicked Herod slightly with his heels and they started off.

"Goodbye! God bless you and keep you!" Bertie's father called softly.

"And your little one," said her mother.

Their unfinished house rose in the darkness on the left, its white boards gleaming in the starlight, as they rode past it. In another month they would have moved in. Mr. Meyer and Anton had worked from sunrise until long past dark day after day, and now their wheat and rye stood tall, ready for harvest, and their corn was already waist-high.

Bertie wept helplessly with pain and with disappointment. She prayed she could bring a healthy baby back to their farm, and that they could all enjoy the harvest together. But musket fire intruded on her prayers, and after that she only endured the long, dark hours of that night.

She was grateful for Anton's quiet strength and even for Herod's disdainful arrogance. No one but Anton could handle his lively, headstrong stallion. But on a night like this one, with gunfire puncturing the soft, black breeze, a horse like Herod, with a rider like Anton, was a comfort indeed.

Just before sunrise they rode through cattle and pigs in the clearing outside Fort Liberty and then through the gate of the stockade. Inside the fort, dawn revealed a chaos of soldiers, of new arrivals trying to find shelter — or at least a small patch of ground for themselves, and of older inhabitants of the Fort streaming out of their cramped quarters in response to an increasing awareness of musket fire. Musket fire that now seemed to be coming from all directions.

Anton helped Bertie down. "What's happened to Colonel George Rogers Clark?" he asked a young soldier who checked them in. "We heard he was coming through area, with a fair-sized group, to secure it for settlers." The youth had no uniform, except for a dirty white dress jacket from the uniform of the Continental Army.

"I guess he is," the young man replied. "But he's securing only the major forts. He hopes that will discourage attacks on smaller ones like ours. He can't cover all the stations and forts, at least not yet. We'll have to fight this one out ourselves. Or come to some kind of agreement with those fellows out there. Our scouts tell us there are British officers in charge outside Fort Liberty, so we may be able to negotiate with them."

"Then there will be an attack?" Bertie asked.

"We're under attack now, ma'am," the soldier said. "You were lucky to get through."

Bertie moaned as her pains began in earnest. Anton called to a young woman who was passing by.

"Ma'am," he said, "could you give my wife some assistance?"

The young woman peered at Bertie through the early morning light. "Come with me," she said to Bertie in German. Then she picked up Bertie's featherbed and helped her through a doorway.

Dust from an earth floor and smoke from a fireplace hung heavy in the air inside the big, low-ceilinged room. Bertie and the German woman stepped over sleeping children and around the children's parents, most of whom were sitting hunched over on bundles of clothing. A woman near the door, holding a screaming, feverish baby, was sobbing quietly as she rocked back and forth. The fetid, dusty air made Bertie feel like vomiting.

Next to the fire lay a young woman with her arm around a tiny, sleeping baby wrapped in a shawl. She could not have been more than fifteen years old, Bertie thought, with her big, frightened eyes and her long red braids.

But then the girl smiled faintly at Bertie. ''Ma's still got some tea. That'll help you through the worst of it,'' she said. Next to the girl stood a woman with strands of red hair creeping out from under a knit cap. She was drinking from a tin cup.

''Sure and I've got just the tea for you, my girl,'' the woman said. ''Now try a sip or two, and then I'll take you back to the Commandant's quarters. That's where my Bridget gave birth to a fine young lad not an hour ago. My tea will relax you.''

Bertie accepted the proferred cup and looked at it with distaste. The woman's hands were dirty and so was the cup. But Bertie had no strength left to refuse help of any kind. She only wanted the next hours to be over.

Just for an instant she considered running back outside to Anton, and she even turned her body awkwardly toward the door. Then she remembered her mother's words about a woman's strength. Maybe this ordeal was even harder for Anton. Now *he* could do nothing but wait. At least she could leave him alone, and she could try to help hurry the birth, since the red haired woman said the tea would do that for her.

Bertie held her breath and took a gulp. The hot liquid burned down her throat and through her chest. The drink was not tea! — it was a toddy, a strong mixture of tea and corn whiskey.

She protested weakly, but then her head began to swim. She welcomed the arms of her two new friends around her waist as they began to guide her toward an open door across the room.

"Hurry! Hurry!" she moaned.

CHAPTER 11

WHEN BERTIE WOKE she was lying on a narrow bed. Through a small window high above her head she could see sunlight. From the angle of the sun she thought it must be early in the forenoon. Why was she lying on a bed in this strange room?

Slowly she became aware of a rough, woolen blanket wrapped around her body, a blanket that smelled of tobacco smoke, and then of a desk and a chair in the center of the little room. She was still in the Commandant's quarters. She moved her hand slowly down across her body. And at once she began to remember.

Bertie looked wildly about the room. She thought she recalled hearing the Irish woman saying to the German, "That toddy always can be trusted to keep a person asleep when it's all over, too. We'll just let her rest an hour, poor thing. You'd best go out now and tell her husband. Tell him to wait a while before he comes back in here, though. I'll finish clearing up."

Poor thing? What had the woman meant? Where was her baby? Bertie thought she recalled the German woman's smile and her saying, "It's a lovely little girl, Meine Frau." But where was the baby?

Now she began to be aware of shouting and confusion outside the Commandant's room. She must get out there to find Anton. Anton would know what to do.

Just when she started to raise herself off the bed, the door opened slightly. The German woman peered inside, and then she shut the door again. Surely she had seen that Bertie was awake.

Bertie sank back and closed her eyes. Tears streamed down her cheeks. Her head was swimming. "I can't face Anton just yet," she thought. "I can't talk to him yet about losing our baby."

The turmoil outside must have covered sounds of Anton's entrance, because when Bertie opened her eyes again, he was standing by her bed. In his arms he held a small bundle. A quiet bundle.

But he smiled at her. "Are you all right, little mother?" he asked.

"Oh, Anton," she said, "I'm so sorry."

"Sorry?" Anton went on smiling. "What can anybody be sorry about this morning, Bertie? I wanted to bring our baby to you myself. I wanted these first minutes alone with you, in spite of that mess outside. But I didn't think you'd wake up so soon."

Bertie could find no words. Whatever did he mean?

"I am mighty glad she came into the world so fast, Bertie. Mrs. Hazen said she'd never seen such a quick birth. Now are you ready to look at our beautiful little fraulein?"

Bertie cried again, with relief. She held out her arms to Anton, and to their baby. "Oh, you must let me hold her, too," she said.

"Mrs. Hazen brought her out to me," Anton said. "She told me you would more than likely sleep for an hour or two. So I have had the baby to myself there by the fire. Bertie, I wish your mother and father could see her. Isn't she a pretty one?"

Bertie thought she really was perfect, albeit perfectly quiet, too. "Has she slept like this all the while?" she asked, gazing down at the sleeping child in her arms.

"Even with the yelling going on around us out there," Anton said. "A real little lady."

More than likely, Bertie thought, *the poor baby thing has had to sleep that whiskey off, just the way her mother did. It's a good thing Mama wasn't here this morning, to see the way her grandchild came into the world!*

The three of them spent a few happy moments together. Anton went outside at one point and then came back with a chuck of corn bread and some hot tea. "Compliments of the Commandant, whose name, by the way, is Captain Price," he said. "He will be here to give you his best wishes, too, in a little while. Things are quieter out there just now."

"The Commandant has sent a messenger to ask for terms of surrender from a British officer he's found out is in charge of the Shawnee attack. Captain Price says he can't hold the fort any longer without risking severe losses to people here in his charge, probably as bad as the losses during the last Indian attack two years ago."

Bertie was apprehensive. "What happens after a surrender, Anton?" she asked. "Tell me the truth. Don't try to shield me. I have to know." Visions of atrocities she had heard about during the last year swam through her brain.

Anton took her hand. "I don't know," he said. "I honestly don't know. But I hope he can come to terms with the Indians, even if it means closing Fort Liberty temporarily. And then we will all be able to go home. When Colonel Clark finally secures this whole area, the fort can open again. It's happened before. It's all a part of settling this land. We'll have to come to some agreement with the Indians."

The door opened and the Commandant came

in. Noise and dust and odors from the big room outside intruded briefly and then were shut off.

"May I offer my congratulations and best wishes, ma'am?" Captain Price began. It was evident that the man was exhausted. His stained and patched uniform was already blotched with perspiration from the warm morning. He had not combed his full white beard and grizzled hair that fell to his shoulders from beneath his hat. He came over to Bertie and leaned down to see the baby, pulling the shawl back from her tiny face. For the first time the baby stirred and began to whimper. The little sound rose like music to Bertie's ears. It was the first sound she had heard from her daughter.

Captain Price smiled a weary smile. "I have three of my own back in Pennsylvania, ma'am," he said. "I've not seen them for two years. In the midst of death, it's good to see life beginning, too."

"Death," Bertie said quietly. "Do you fear we are all going to die, then?"

He was silent for a moment. "If my plans work out, we won't," he said. "We're playing a game of chess with the British, and I've made my move. Even if I have only a pawn to move, I'm giving it a try."

Bertie spent the afternoon in the Commandant's room, dozing. Toward evening Anton helped her to move into a storeroom, where he had piled hemp mats, with her featherbed atop them. Most of the tools and kegs of ammunition stored there had been taken out. The tiny room was hot and stuffy, but she had some privacy.

After Anton left to find Captain Price and offer his help, Bertie held her sleeping baby and hummed an old German lullaby she remembered from her childhood. It was a prayer for an infant's blest sleep.

After a while the German woman came to see her with her two small boys. It looked as though both of the boys would grow up to be big and broad like their mother. Like her they had black hair and round dark eyes.

"My kinder have been begging to get a peep at your little one," the woman said. "My name, by the way," she went on, with a smile, "is Frau Hazen. It's time we became acquainted."

Bertie smiled, too. "How kind you've been to us," she said. She drew the shawl back so the boys could see the baby.

"I did wonder if I could help you start to take care of your baby, meine Frau. Mrs. O'Haire is anxious to be of help, too, but I am not sure I would always accept her advice, especially in matters of medication."

"You're remembering the toddy?" Bertie asked. "I must say I'd have to agree with you."

"I would not try such a thing again, my child. Not ever," Mrs. Hazen said. "I'm convinced you are lucky you both survived. Mrs. O'Haire's daughter is not doing well at all, and neither is her child."

"Oh, do ask Mrs. O'Haire to bring her daughter in here with me," Bertie said. "Is the girl still out in that dirty spot by the fireplace?"

Mrs. Hazen looked at her quietly for a moment. Then she said, "I believe we should talk such a move over with your husband. Herr Marx is quite disturbed over the whiskey Mrs. O'Haire gave you. At first he was afraid your baby had been harmed."

Bertie smiled. "My husband can trust me now to look for our baby," she said. "And I believe he's standing guard duty this evening, so please don't disturb him. Just ask the O'Haires to spend the night here with me, won't you? The daughter and her baby, that is. And if you and your boys can find a place to stretch out on your blankets in here, why don't you stay with me, too?"

The German woman looked doubtful. "Without your husband's consent first?" she asked.

"With *my* consent, Bertie said firmly.

Bertie's night was long. She continued to be anxious about her sleeping baby. The darkness outside spawned scattered episodes of shooting, and even more ominous times of silence. But inside her tiny, hot room, there was comfort, somehow, in sharing a precarious existence with all of these children. Children who would, God willing, grow up to dwell in this land.

When Anton came in to her after his guard duty was finished, he carefully eased himself down beside her on the featherbed. With his arms around her, Bertie finally went to sleep.

CHAPTER 12

BERTIE SPENT THREE MORE days in the little storage room. The baby whom she and Anton decided to call Adelheit, after Bertie's mother, soon began to assert her identity. She squirmed and cried enough to satisfy her parents that she would grow up to become a normal, healthy child.

Bridget's baby, however, lay pale and quiet in her mother's arms, though Bridget was lively and talkative. Her constant chatter wearied Bertie. They cared for their babies together, with welcome advice from Mrs. Hazen. Bridget's mother came in to see her grandchild only once in a while, for she was busy looking after her two younger children who, Mrs. Hazen told them, now roamed about inside the stockade teasing the soldiers and generally making a nuisance of themselves. They did entertain her own little boys now and then, though, Mrs. Hazen said, with games of hide and seek.

"My father, you know, had his scalp taken by the Shawnee three years back," Bridget said, one day after Mrs. Hazen had gone out, having told the young women to take a nap, "and they left him for dead, poor man. It was I who found him, and me only twelve at the time. But then he lived on. Not the man he was, of course, sick often with fever and with other maladies. We could not have survived, I think, if our kind of neighbor, Mr. Metzler, had not come to our aid. Then after we buried our father last summer, Mr. Metzler and I were wed."

"Is he here now, in the fort?" Bertie asked.

"Oh, no," Bridget said. "He brought us to the gate, but then he went back to our farm. He'd raised it from an Irish tenant's kind of farm to a German landowner's estate, he said, and no Indian was going to take it away from him! He'll come for us, just you see, as soon as our soldiers scare the savages off."

Bertie wished she could have such confidence in the poorly-equipped and poorly-trained young men who were trying to defend the fort. Anton had told her that supplies of ammunition were running low, and there was very little food left. They had walked for a few minutes together the night before along a short corridor that led into the few rooms built along one side of the fort.

Fragrant June air was welcome after her days in the stuffy room. There was little activity now among the sleeping inhabitants of the fort. Beyond its walls cows bellowed. Soldiers sometimes sneaked out to milk the cows under cover of darkness. That was risky business, though. One man had been wounded by gunfire out of the forest the night before when he went out to tend some of the livestock that had not wandered away from the fort.

"The British officer, Colonel Bond, only laughed at the soldiers we sent out to him to ask about terms of surrender," Anton had told her. "Our scouts say there are at least four Indian tribes in the hills out there now. And more of them come into our area every day. Chief Dragging Canoe, a Cherokee, once said this would be a 'dark and bloody ground.'"

As depressing as Anton's news was, Bertie was glad he felt he could share it with her. "Does Captain Price have any other plans to try to save the fort?" she asked.

"I understand there will be a parley tomorrow, here inside the fort. Colonel Bond will be here himself. At least we can see what he looks like."

"Anton, why are the British coming down among the Indians in Kentucke? British interests are far to the north of Kentucke, aren't they?"

"It's a new strategy, I think. Instead of paying bounty only for scalps, these days the British are paying ransom for live settlers brought up to

Detroit. A good many Indians are happy to get white men out of their land, on any terms."

"And then what will the British expect of hostages that have been ransomed off in Detroit?"

Anton paused before he answered. "Loyalty, I suppose," he finally said. "And thanks for saving our scalps, and the scalps of our children. The alternative, if Fort Liberty were to fall, I'm afraid would not be pleasant."

During the rest of that night, while Anton was on guard duty, Bertie's visions of the future were not pleasant, either. She turned thankfully to a matter at hand. Her little girl was hungry. Across the room Bridget slept quietly on her blanket, her arm around her sickly child.

On the fourth morning, Bertie was feeling remarkably good. She and Bridget went out to watch the arrival of the British officer. Inside the fort all of its inhabitants were waiting in the yard with obvious apprehension while one of the soldiers opened the gate. She noticed that Rev. Burns had come into the fort, too. He was standing next to the gate. It was good to see a friend among all of these strangers.

Colonel Bond's red coat and gold braid shone in the sun when he rode through the gate of the stockade. Walking alongside his horse were two Shawnee chiefs. Their great headdresses of eagle feathers made an impressive sight. When they came to a halt the Indians held their muskets in both hands, ready for any emergency. Through the gate Bertie could see other Indians standing in the clearing in groups, all of them concentrating on searching this way and that for any problems that might arise beyond the open gate.

Colonel Bond dismounted. He and Captain Price saluted and then they began to talk, but Bertie could not hear what they were saying. Anton stood with a group of soldiers near the officers, so Bertie knew she would have an account of the negotiations later.

After a half hour, with no evident signs of progress between the men, several children were beginning to get restless. They started to wander among the crowd. Some of them were crying.

"They're hungry, the poor things. My brothers are hungry, too, I know. We've got to do something, Bertie," Bridget said. "I've got an idea. Come along with me, over to the other side of the fort."

But as soon as they turned around, one of the Indians moved. Within an instant he blocked their exit. He held his gun like a barrier in front of him.

Colonel Bond saw what the Indian had done. "We'd rather you didn't leave, ladies," he called to them. "No one is to leave until I give the word."

When Bridget saw the musket thrust in front of her, she gasped and stood motionless. Bertie remembered the story about what Indians had done to the girl's father. Any action would be up to her. Bertie took a deep breath, and then she eased herself around the gun and walked slowly over to the British officer. "We meant no harm, Colonel Bond," she said. "Mrs. Metzler and I both have small babies to care for in a room back there. It seems as though it might be some time before you and Captain Price are finished talking, or we would we bring them out here with us." She smiled up at him. "The sun, though, is hot on the head of a tiny baby. Might we walk back to our room and look after our children? We would be much obliged."

Colonel Bond stared at her for a moment. He was a young man, with a strong chin and arrogant blue eyes. "Go ahead then, ma'am," he said. "But don't attempt any tricks." Then he gestured for the Indian to come back to his side.

Bridget led Bertie to the other end of the fort, where a spring bubbled up next to a small back door. Next to the stones around the spring stood a wooden bucket. "Aren't we going to check the babies?" Bertie asked.

"Later," Bridget said. She opened the tiny door and peered out. "I thought so," she said. "Everybody's on the other side. Just listen to that cow beller! She's got to be milked!"

Bridget slipped outside. There was no movement from the forest beyond the clearing. Three lowing cows were walking around near the stockade, hoping their owners would come out and attend to them.

While Bertie watched nervously, Bridget did a quick job of crouching down and milking the three cows. In spite of her apprehension Bertie could hardly keep from laughing while she watched the red pigtails flying from one cow to another.

Then someone in the forest must have seen the girl. A bullet whizzed past her ear. At once she was up and on her way back into the fort. But the bucket of milk was safe, and so was Bridget.

Bertie quickly closed the gate while Bridget sped along the stockade fence and into their tiny storeroom. Bertie just made it to the door before the Indian found her. He grabbed her arm and started to drag her back toward the crowd, but then Bridget appeared in the doorway with both babies, who were crying fretfully.

"Now look what you've done!" she scolded. "Wait until I tell Colonel Bond!"

"Shooting!" the Indian said.

"Shooting? We heard it, too. Can't you keep your people quiet? Maybe somebody shot at a rabbit."

The Indian released Bertie. He gestured, "Come with me." They followed him back to the crowd in the yard, carrying their babies. Bridget giggled, and then she whispered, "My brothers and the Hazen boys won't go hungry tonight!"

The officers in the center of the crowd were now talking and waving their arms — and their fists — at each other. They took no notice of Bertie and Bridget.

CHAPTER 13

THE SUN WAS indeed hot on the babies' heads. Now several more children were whining or sobbing quietly while they sat in the dust at their parents' feet. Most of the children had gone without much food for the last day or two, and they were restless and irritable. Near Bertie an old woman, leaning on her stick, began to mutter loudly to herself. Her daughter tried to hush her.

Bertie wrinkled her nose. Along with the midday heat and a press of sweaty bodies was added a growing, almost palpable tension, a desire for *any* kind of resolution to the settlers' worries of the past few days.

"If that bunch of decorated peacocks over there don't go away and leave us alone soon, I guess I'll have to try another trick," Bridget whispered. "My little one is drooping in this heat like a wilted daisy."

Bertie, holding Adelheit close and humming softly to her whimpering baby, glanced at Bridget's little boy. His tiny face was pale and lifeless beneath its fringe of red hair.

Then finally Colonel Bond and Captain Prince saluted each other again. At once the Englishman mounted his horse and turned it toward the gate.

The two Shawnees, before they followed him, looked the crowd over and slowly appraised what they saw, scrutinizing one settler after another. Then, with a kind of solemn flourish, they wheeled and strode through the gate behind Colonel Bond's horse.

Bertie shivered. *They looked as though they were counting scalps,* she thought.

Everyone crowded closer to Captain Price. A soldier brought a bucket for him to stand on, and he looked out gravely at his audience before he began to speak.

"Well, my friends," he said, "we have reached an understanding. I believe I have been able to persuade Colonel Bond that there are a good many people here in Fort Liberty who are loyal to King George of England. He agreed that it would not be wise to allow hostile local Indians to slaughter all of the inhabitants that have been under my protection."

A young woman standing at the edge of the crowd screamed. Bertie looked over at her, noting that her pregnancy was far advanced. Bertie whispered a prayer of thanks for Adelheit's safe delivery, and for her own fast recovery.

Captain Price paused for a moment. "I'm sorry to have to speak of these matters, ma'am," he said, "but it is best for all of you — even the little children — to know what lies ahead for us.

"Colonel Bond tells me that most of the Indians surrounding the fort are Hurons he brought with him from the Detroit area. The British are offering ransom for every person from Kentucke the Indians can safely bring to Detroit. There was no talk about violence, only about means of transporting all of us to British-held territory in the North. There are river routes and overland trails we will have to follow. It will be a long, hard journey."

An old man with a full, white beard asked, "And then it is true that we will not be allowed to go back peacefuly to the good soil we have tilled during these hard years, is it not?"

"I'm afraid you're right," Captain Price said, sadly. "I've grown to love this land, too. But there was no mention of allowing us to stay here. Not now."

Rev. Burns called out, "What did the Shawnee chiefs have to say? It is the Shawnees' land we are farming. It is they who are angry. Did the chiefs agree with Colonel Bond?"

Captain Price cleared his throat. "That was what we talked about most of the time. All of you are aware of the reputation of the British officer who has been encouraging violence throughout the Western lands around us. And you have a right to be worried about what might happen with this officer in charge of the siege. In the end, though, he said he could assure me that the people inside the fort would have his full protection. Colonel Bond has twenty-five men of his own outside the fort, and a hundred Indians from the North."

"And when will we have to open the gate to the savages?" Rev. Burns asked. "I've heard a rumor that there is no more gunpowder in the fort. And that the British have just placed a cannon outside. Is that right?"

"Yes, Reverend Burns," Captain Price said. "You've heard that story correctly."

Anton, who had moved over to Bertie's side, called out, "But if you decide we should still make a stand, we will. You can count on me, my friend."

Captain Price smiled, a grim smile. "Spoken like a true soldier," he said. "It may well be because of the few men like you that we have living inside this fort today, Mr. Marx, that our lives are being spared. Colonel Bond has heard about you, and he considers you to be loyal to King George. And he would be hard put, he says, to try to sort out Rebels from Patriots."

Everyone turned to look at Anton. He said nothing, but Bertie saw him press his lips together, and then the muscles in his cheek and neck tightened. Although many of the local people probably preferred British rule to a precarious future outside of that rule, the settlers considered it foolish, so far away from actual battles, to show a firm allegiance to either side.

Bertie was annoyed. She wondered how much more Anton would have to do to prove that he was dependable. In the eyes of the settlers he was still a Hessian soldier, one of those outsiders who were brought into the country by King George to fight as mercenaries. He was someone whose services could be bought.

A good many rumors had come to Bertie, through Bridget and her mother, centering on the fact that a lot of people felt Anton Marx could not be trusted, when trust in each other was all they had left.

CHAPTER 14

A LATE AFTERNOON THUNDERSTORM had drenched the settlers and trappers and soldiers huddled in the clearing inside Fort Liberty. The early evening air was a little fresher now, but thunderheads still lingered above the horizon. It looked as though it might rain again.

Bertie and Anton stood beneath one of the corner sentry boxes. Anton was holding Adelheit, singing softly to her. "Well, my tiny fraulein," he sang, "the tales we will have to tell you, when you grow up to be a pretty frau like your mama! Perhaps we should tell you lies — never would you believe our true stories!"

Bertie was tense. Her ears were listening for any threatening sounds from the forest, now ringing only with evening bird calls. But Anton's words made her laugh, and for just a moment she forgot the next day's ominous promise of tears and hardship.

"There'll be little sleeping here tonight," she said. "I'm glad the children had a few swallows of milk. They might get some rest, with the comfort of a bit of milk in their stomachs."

All around, people were gathered into small groups, talking quietly. Across the clearing the Reverend Burns was leading a few settlers in prayer. The women, who usually went into the big central room to sleep, were still outside. Beyond the pallisade, cows bellowed, and now and then a horse neighed.

"Anton," Bertie said, "what will happen to Herod? Do you think they'll let you ride him north?"

Anton's face was grim. "I couldn't bring myself to talk about that problem," he said, "even to you. But I've taken care of it."

His look was so forbidding Bertie hesitated to go on, but she had to know. "What do you mean?" she asked.

Anton sighed, and then he handed the sleeping baby back to Bertie. "I've never been one to talk about things that give me trouble," he said. "It's just not in me to talk about the way I feel."

Bertie knew that was true. How well she knew. "But if you don't tell me about Herod, I'll only worry about him," she said.

Anton turned away, with an impatient fling of his arm. In the dusk she could hardly make out the expression on his face, but his body spoke of weariness, and of anger.

"I've gone out every night to check on Herod," he said. "Since we got here I kept him tethered in a place far off the trails. In the night I would take him to water. And then I would ride. Riding him at night helped me get through the days, Bertie, because I knew all along how it would have to end. I knew I could never allow a Shawnee to sit on Herod's back."

Bertie drew a quick breath. "Oh, Anton," she said, tears coming to her eyes. She reached for his hand and found a fist, a fist that gave no response to her.

"Was . . . was last night the last time?" she asked. "Or are you going out tonight?"

"Last night," he answered. "With all the gunfire around us, I thought it would sound like just one more shot somewhere in the forest. I knew tonight would be a quiet one."

His hand finally relaxed, and he returned her grasp. "After all," he said, "in the light of what's happening to a good many of these people here in the fort, that's all it was. Just one more shot."

Bertie put her arms around him. She held him close, with the baby between them. A terrible thought registered in her brain. *Maybe this is the last time you will hold him,* it said. *Maybe this is the end of your youth. Of your happiness.*

She shook her head to clear away the fright

and looked up at Anton. If he felt that way, too, he gave no sign. But he kept his arms around her and Adelheit in an almost savage possessiveness.

"Say your prayers tonight, Bertie," he said. "And say them for me, too. I'm not even good at telling God what I'd probably like to say. It's only childish prayers that come out of my mouth, and then I feel childish, too."

She held him close for a few more precious moments.

Gradually, one woman after another began to head for the big low-ceilinged building in the center of the fort. Several of them carried sleeping children. Soft good-nights and a "Come and wake me before dawn" floated on the warm air. Whiffs of tobacco smoke mingled with smells of perspiring people who had been trapped together for days inside the small enclosure.

Bertie was thankful Anton had found the tiny store room for her, but she felt a little guilty, too, knowing that now there were old women and sick children who would have welcomed the privacy and relatively clean air she and Bridget and Frau Hazen enjoyed.

Then Bertie heard Bridget's voice close to them in the darkness. "I'll go inside, Bertie," she said. "Ma's trying to settle the boys down. Those two are real rascals, to be sure. Mrs. Hazen and her little ones are already asleep, I guess. The gentlemen say we'll all have a lot of walking to do tomorrow. Do you think that's so, Mr. Marx?"

"I don't know, Mrs. Metzler," Anton said. "I'd be lying to you if I told you anything different." He paused but then he chuckled and went on, "I do think we'll all have a chance to look at life from a way we never did before. And I'll bet you're game, even for that. The Irish have always had to put up with a lot of troubles, and they usually live to joke about it."

Bridget's voice came back out of the dark. "That's what my Pa always said. And I believed him. But now," the voice faltered, "but now I've got my baby to carry all the way to Detroit. My sick little baby. And I have to leave my good husband behind. I fear I can't think of any old family jokes to cheer me up tonight." She turned away and headed for the storeroom.

Bertie said a quick prayer for her own parents. For her father, who had stayed to guard the farm, and for her mother, who would always stand by him.

"Anton," Bertie said, "I want to stay out here with you."

Just then a roll of thunder sounded overhead. Lightning flashes she had been trying to ignore were coming closer. One illuminated their faces before it struck a tree in the forest just beyond the wall of the fort. There was a sound of limbs crashing and then another thunder clap.

Anton put his arm around her again as the rain began to fall. "I wish you could, Bertie. I think I should stay here, but you should get Adelheit inside."

Bertie knew he was right. "Yes, you're right. Come to us if you can."

The downpour made their leaving easier, because there was no time to linger. Anton's last words followed her though the darkness. "Take care of our little fraulein," he said.

CHAPTER 15

BERTIE STEPPED CAREFULLY OVER the sleeping Hazen children. In the darkness she sensed the presense of their small bodies lying in their usual places, and she sensed, too, the fact that the two women in the room were not asleep. "It's me," she whispered. "Another storm's coming."

"I hope the rain's over before we have to begin our walk toward Detroit in the morning," Bridget said softly.

"I'm praying my man won't take it into his head to try to reach the fort," Mrs. Hazen said, in German. "If the wheat is finally harvested by now, he may try and find a way to get through to us. I pray the Lord will keep him safe back there in our good house."

The women did not speak again, but Bertie knew none of them would get much sleep. She held Adelheit close, and then she settled down as well as she could on her pile of hemp rugs, in the now stifling little room.

From time to time Bertie drifted off into a restless doze. All at once a great clamor woke her. Her sleepy brain said, "More thunder." But then suddenly she was wide awake.

Screams and scuffling and terrible thuds had awakened her. Not thunder. In the darkness close to her ear she heard Bridget's low voice in prayer. Bertie sprang up to try to open the door but found Mrs. Hazen blocking her way. "It's best to stay here," Mrs. Hazen whispered. "Letting the savages know where we are would do us no good."

"But Anton's out there!" Bertie cried.

"And so are my mother and my brothers," Bridget said. She paused, and then she went on in a tense voice that was barely in control, "Sad to say, though, Mrs. Hazen is right. We can do our dear ones no good by running out there like fools and getting ourselves killed."

By now the noise outside had awakened the sleeping boys. "What is it, Mama?" the older one asked. At once Mrs. Hazen rushed to them with a soothing, "Hush now. It will all be over soon." Bertie slid into Mrs. Hazen's place in front of the door. She held Adelheit tightly in her arms, her own big shawl around both of them.

With her ear against the door, Bertie tried to follow the course of the melée outside. Women and children were screaming in the courtyard amid sounds of thumping and horrible whoops of rage and of what often sounded to her like yells of elation. It seemed to go one for an eternity.

Then all at once she heard sounds of feet rushing through the little hallway outside the storeroom. And then they rushed back. The sounds of feet in moccasins.

Bridget edged up to the door. "Bertie," she whispered. "They don't know about this room yet. Before they start to make a search, let's try to slip out that back gate."

Mrs. Hazen, not able to understand Bridget's rapid English, said, "No! No! Whatever she says, no. We must stay here where it is safe."

"What did she say?" Bridget asked. Apparently she understood only Mrs. Hazen's "Nein! Nein!"

"She thinks we'll be safer here," Bertie said. She listened at the door again. It was quiet outside now. A man in the courtyard was shouting something in English.

"Well, I don't intend to wait," Bridget said. "Let me past. I'm going out the back way before it starts up again. I'd rather die on my feet than die cowering here in a corner."

"I'll go with you," Bertie said. She reached for a small bag of clothing wrapped in an old shawl she kept at the end of her hemp bed. Then they opened the door to darkness that was only a little less intense because there were glimpses of flaming, smoky flares coming from the other side of the courtyard, beyond the commandant's quarters.

"Good-by, Mrs. Hazen," Bertie whispered. "May the Lord bless you. And bless your boys, too."

Bertie and Bridget ran along the storage area until they had to cross an open space that circled the spring. The gate behind the spring was ajar, and Bridget gave it a little push. Suddenly she screamed.

Bertie felt a great, rough hand grasp her shoulder, and her heart seemed to leap into her throat. Bridget's quick gasp told her she had been stopped, too.

But an instant later Bertie caught her breath with relief. The arm that held her was not bare, but covered with a uniform, undoubtedly a British uniform. It felt crisp and new, not like the ragged, washed-out uniforms of the soldiers stationed at the fort.

Sounds of feet pounded toward them on the rain-soaked clay. But the sounds stopped outside the little storeroom where they had been sleeping. A moment later there was a woman's voice crying out and then mingled screams of children. And then the terrible sounds of blows. Blows that abruptly ended the screaming.

Through her own sobs Bertie became aware of Bridget's wailing, "Holy mother of God, protect us!"

Then the footsteps came pounding toward them again. "Stand still," their captor ordered, releasing his hold on them. Bertie hugged her whimpering baby more tightly and backed up against the stockade wall. She could make out the shadowy form of the British soldier when he swung his rifle into position. He gave an order in a language she did not understand, and the footsteps halted.

At once the soldier rushed over toward the Indian and began to shout at him.

Bertie felt Bridget huddling close to her. She dropped her bundle of clothing and put her arm around the girl. From Bridget's baby rose a thin, sickly wail.

"Bertie," Bridget whispered, "do you suppose the savages," she paused and whispered softly, "violate women?"

"Hush," she said, trying to comfort Bridget, "don't beg for troubles before they get here."

"Well, I won't give up my life or my baby's life, without making one of those savages pay dearly." She sighed. "Poor, poor Mrs. Hazen," she added, her voice breaking.

The soldier returned. "Don't try any more tricks," he said to them. "I've got to stand guard at this gate, so you will both be obliged to stay here with me. Anyway," he added, "I have little doubt you will wander away, knowing the Indians wait for you out there in the courtyard."

CHAPTER 16

IT WAS QUIET NOW on the other side of the fort, except for an occasional groan. A child cried out, "Mama! Where are you, Mama?" And then "Papa?"

The heavy, fragrant darkness stifled Bertie. If only she could move, if only she could stealthily follow that Indian's route between the store room and the commandant's quarters to a scene she knew would be almost too much to bear. But what she might find out there could be no worse than what she pictured in her mind. "Anton," she murmured. "Oh, Anton, where are you?"

The gruff British voice at once growled, "Quiet!" Bertie choked back her sobs. It was Adelheit she had to think about now. She had promised Anton she would take care of their little fraulein. She hugged her baby close to her.

A few minutes later heavy footsteps approached. A big form emerged from the darkness and then another British voice said, "Lock that gate, soldier. Everything's secure in here now, I guess. There's an awful mess, though."

Their captor locked the gate. "What happened, sir?" he asked. "Can't the Colonel control his Red Indians?" He turned Bertie and Bridget toward the front of the fort and gave them a little push. "These two tried to sneak out the back way, and they almost ran into real trouble," he added.

The men walked behind them. Bertie got a whiff of spilled blood in the warm air when they passed their little storage room, and suddenly she felt her eyes fill again. Next to her, Bridget was murmuring to herself.

"Don't let what you see here upset you, ladies. No more shrieking, please," their captor said when they reached the courtyard. "There's nothing can be done. It wasn't what we wanted, either. Just walk on through and out that gate."

Someone had left a flare on a post next to the front entrance. Its flickering light revealed bodies lying here and there in terrible postures. Someone was moaning. It was dark beyond the reaches of the torch, and as hard as she tried, Bertie could make out no form or clothing she recognized. When Bridget made a quick break toward a quiet heap dressed in a long, dark skirt, their captor caught her shoulder again and turned her toward the gate.

In the clearing outside, soldiers were directing groups of settlers toward a path through the forest. Sounds of shouted orders in English and in an Indian tongue mingled with sounds of shuffling feet and anxious exchanges in both English and German. Flares revealed haggard faces of the prisoners. Bertie noted with some alarm that all the prisoners seemed to be women and children. Several women without children were crying. She was afraid to speak to their British captor, but she had to find out. "Why are there no men here?" she asked. "Have the Indians," she whispered the word, "*murdered* all the men?"

"I don't know. I was stationed there at the back," he said, "but killing was not our plan. Our orders are to bring settlers from Kentucke to Detroit for ransom. There was no plan for killing." He paused, apparently considering for the first time her concern about someone she loved. "It may be the person you want to find has gone on ahead, ma'am," he finally said. "I believe the men will be obliged to walk, but the plan is to take the rest of you on river routes."

Bertie closed her eyes. "Dear God," she said. She could pray no more; the worry was too deep for words, but in her heart she felt grateful for that bit of hope to hold onto.

After a few moments she looked curiously at the beardless face of the tall, young man who held her captive. In the flickering light he appeared imposing in his red coat, but she now saw that he was probably no older than she. Anton might well have been a comrade of this boy at one time. Had Anton ever supervised such carnage as this while he was a soldier?

Bridget stood quietly nearby, her face bleak. Bertie took her hand. "That soldier says most people have gone on ahead," she said. "Maybe Anton and your mother and brothers are already on their way."

Bridget did not respond, she only stared into the darkness. "Even if the children survived that horror," she finally said, "just think what they have had to watch. Think what they have had to hear. It would be enough to bend their brains out of shape for sure."

In her mind Bertie had to agree, but she said, "It was dark, Bridget. It was terrible, but it was dark. Maybe it was just all confusion for them. Besides," she added, squeezing the girl's limp hand, "children do pop back. You did."

Bridget pulled her hand and away and put both arms around her baby. "No, I didn't," she said. "And I never will."

While they had been talking, soldiers had brought others to become a part of their little group. Bertie counted nine or ten women and several small children. Then their captor pointed at four Indians who were standing at the edge of the clearing. "Those!" he shouted to an officer who seemed to be sorting out settlers and making plans for them. "And," he called, "I'd better take that pastor along, too. If I've got to do this by myself, I can use another pair of arms I'll be able to count on."

Then out from the crowd of settlers and traders strode Reverend Burns. For Bertie, only one person could have been more welcome. At least she would have someone to lean on during the terrible ordeal ahead.

CHAPTER 17

A HOT SUMMER SUN had climbed halfway up the sky before Bertie and her weary companions reached the river. Above the eastern hills, banks of clouds that had given the captives a stormy night were now traveling over distant forests and over other settlers waiting with apprehension for an Indian attack. News of the fall of the fort surely must have spread rapidly throughout the whole area, sometimes meeting news equally dreadful from other stations and forts.

Bertie was exhausted. She had carried Adelheit and her little bag of clothing along the trail that led to the river for several hours. They had stopped walking only once. When they stopped, the British soldier brought out a few small loaves of bread made from corn, or "maize," as the British called it after an Indian word. Everyone tore off a chunk of bread, and the women, who had been carrying their weary children, fed them silently. The whole group was tense with choked-back terror.

While they had been resting for a few minutes in the forest, Bertie had hoped she might be able to change the baby's soiled clothing when they reached the river. Now at last the morning sun was glinting on the gray waters before them.

"We'll stop here until the sun is at its zenith," the soldier who was in charge of the travelers announced. "I am Sergeant Russell, and I can assure you there will be no more violence. You will be under my protection for the rest of the journey."

At once a few women sank onto the warm river bank. Two little boys ran to the edge of the water and began to drink, cupping water in their hands and slurping loudly. Then they laughed and splashed each other.

Bertie saw Bridget watching the boys. The girl's eyes were red from crying and from fatigue. *I pray Bridget's brothers are just as lively somewhere else on this river,* she thought. Then she walked down along the bank, below the spot where people were drinking and splashing water on their faces. She washed out Adelheit's small pieces of laundry and spread the clothing on the grass to dry. Without another glance at the group upstream she stretched out next to her sleeping baby and immediately fell asleep, too.

Shouts of "Wake up, ladies!" awakened Bertie. She lay in the same position in which she had gone to sleep. It seemed as though she had hardly dropped off, but when she managed to open her eyes she saw that the sun was halfway across the sky. Wearily she turned her face toward a group of sleepers a little way up the river.

Abruptly she sat up and stared. At the edge of the water floated a great canoe, larger than any canoe she had known existed. Two of the Indians that Sgt. Russell had picked to come along with them were already sitting in the canoe, one at the front and the other in the stern. Their paddles were in hand, and they gazed impassively at the little group of settlers. The two other Indians held their craft close to the shore. They wore only breechcloths, and bright beaded bands to keep their hair out of their eyes. Sgt. Russell was beginning to direct one or two women toward the canoe.

The old woman who had mumbled loudly to herself at the gathering in the fort the day before — *Can it have been only yesterday?* Bertie thought — leaned heavily on her daughter's arm and put one leg stiffly over the side of the canoe. They both wore black knit scarves on their heads. The old woman had pulled her scarf far over her face, until one could see only the tip of her long nose. Still muttering and complaining loudly as she crouched, she was unable to move any farther.

Then Bertie saw Rev. Burns for the first time that morning. He was kneeling next to one of the women, with his head bowed. But when he heard the old woman and her daughter, who were both screaming and in immediate danger of falling into the water, he got up and ran over to them. "There, there, Mrs. Kotz," he said. He lifted her trembling body the way he would lift a child and, with one foot inside the canoe, set the old woman down carefully on a bag of clothing her daughter had already tossed in.

Bertie waved at Bridget and called her name, but the girl stood woodenly, with her quiet baby in her arms. Only when Sgt. Russell gave her a little shove did she shuffle toward the stern of the canoe, her eyes on the ground in front of her.

By the time Bertie had collected her clean clothing from the grass and put it back into her old shawl, all the others had settled themselves in the canoe. Mothers carried their sleepy children aboard. The children, who would normally feel excitement about riding in an Indian canoe, were numb with exhaustion. Reverend Burns put his hand under Bertie's elbow when she awkwardly lifted her foot over the side, holding Adelheit close to her chest and clutching her bundle of clothing with her other hand.

"Oh, tell me, my friend," she said to him, "did you see my husband last night? I must know. Don't spare me if you have news that is — bad." She whispered the last word.

He looked at her gravely for a moment. "It was too dark to see what happened, Mrs. Marx," he said, finally. He settled himself next to Bertie. Adelheit was crying now, and Bertie tried to quiet her in the limited space she had between the Reverend Burns and an Indian squatting in front of her, facing the captives. In front of him was an Indian paddling in the bow of the canoe.

"But you hesitated before you answered me, Reverend Burns," she insisted. "I must believe you saw *something*."

"Please don't worry," he said. "We will find comfort in prayer for all our lost loved ones."

He grew silent, and Bertie stopped her questions. Soon she began to find some comfort in her contact with this tiny life that needed her, every moment. She began to hum softly to match the rhythm of the paddles, to the rhythm of her own heartbeat.

"I will survive," Bertie vowed. "I will. And so will you, my little fraulein. Until we are all together again."

CHAPTER 18

BEHIND BERTIE OLD MRS. KOTZ muttered and complained. And now Bertie saw that the Indian who faced her was growing annoyed with the shrill, cracked voice. He raised his arm and pointed at the woman.

"You!" he said. "You!"

Reverend Burns turned back to Mrs. Kotz's daughter. "Speak to your mother, ma'am," he whispered. "It will do the rest of us no good to have the savages upset."

"She pays little attention to me," the younger woman said. But she took her mother's withered hands in hers and held them and stroked them gently. For a while the muttering stopped.

A few moments later Bertie, who was just starting to relax, felt a bump, and she realized their canoe had scraped the bottom of the river.

At once two Indians jumped into the water and pulled it to shore. "All out!" shouted Sergeant Russell, and the slow business of getting captives and their bags of clothing out of the canoe began.

Mrs. Kotz shrieked, "What are these savages doing to us now?"

With a quick movement Reverend Burns turned around and lifted her out, and set her on her feet. Then he looked up just in time to see the Indian who had pointed at Mrs. Kotz raise his tomahawk. "No!" he cried, picking the old woman up again and running toward the forest with her. The Indian followed, his tomahawk in the air.

Sergeant Russell stepped in front of Mrs. Kotz's screaming daughter. "Don't go in there, ma'am," he said. "These fellows have been giving us trouble all the way. Let the pastor deal with this problem."

Bertie, her heart pounding, peered into the darkness of the forest. She clutched Adelheit close to her, and then she thought to look back to find out what the other Indians were doing. The two who held the canoe stood quietly, seemingly indifferent to the drama in the forest. But the third strode over to Sergeant Russell and began to shout at him. The shouting was only a word or two, repeated again and again, but to her horror Bertie saw him pointing at Bridget and then at the two little boys. The mothers of the boys watched the Indian's gestures. They picked up their children and held them in their arms. The old woman's exit had happened so quickly that some of the women who had been complaining loudly about being bullied were still unaware of their peril. Their diatribe and the Indian's shouts had covered any sounds from Mrs. Kotz's fate in the forest.

Bertie edged closer to Sergeant Russell, the only possible island of safety. "No!" she heard him say to the Indian. "No scalps!" He made an unmistable gesture with his finger across his forehead. "Scalps: no ransom. Live people: ransom." He pointed at the captives, and then his fingers rubbed imaginary wealth together.

The Indian, his bronze body gleaming in the late afternoon sun, towered over the young Englishman, but the youth kept his rifle ready and stared back, his blue eyes hard and cold.

The Indian finally grunted and turned away. He strode through the frightened group to his fellow comrades at the canoe. They talked quietly for a moment and then the aggressive Indian pointed down river. Immediately the other two lifted the canoe over their heads and began to walk along the bank to the north, to deeper water.

"Move on, now, you people!" the sergeant called. "We can have no invalids. No cripples. And no more complaining. March right along!"

Mrs. Kotz's daughter sank to the ground, weeping. "Kill me, too," she said. "What cruelty I have seen today."

Sergeant Russell turned to Bertie. "Take her with you, ma'am," he said. "If the pastor can save the old lady, he will. There's nothing I can do. I'll have enough trouble keeping the rest of you alive."

"You swore you would protect us. You swore there would be no more killing," Mrs. Kotz's daughter said, tears running down her ashen cheeks. She took a corner of her black knit scarf and wiped her eyes. "God in Heaven, what is to become of us all?"

The other captives had started to walk slowly along the river, as they had been ordered to do. Those with children stayed at the back of the group, nearer to the sergeant than to the Indians. Then out of the forest, now far ahead of them, strode the man who had attacked Mrs. Kotz. He joined the others, but a turn in the river made it impossible for Bertie to see whether or not he carried a new scalp. She suddenly felt as though she would be sick.

Mrs. Kotz's daughter was beginning to develop the look of shock Bridget had worn the night before. Even now Bridget moved in a slow, awkward way that was utterly foreign to the girl Bertie had come to love during these last terrible days.

A moment later she caught a glimpse of Reverend Burns. He was standing a few yards away, under an overhanging limb. He put his finger to his lips and pointed at Sergeant Russell.

Bertie touched Sergeant Russell's sleeve and put her finger on her mouth, too. The youth twisted around with an impatient movement, but then he saw Reverend Burns, and he ran over to him.

Mrs. Kotz's daughter was unaware of anything but her own misery. She sat on the grass and rocked slowly back and forth. She may have been praying, but no sound came from her lips.

Bertie settled Adelheit against her shoulder and sat down next to the woman. She put her arm around her. In the late afternoon stillness, though, Bertie could hear the low conversation behind her. She turned slightly so she could see the men.

"Do you have a shovel, Sergeant Russell?" Reverend Burns asked. "There must be a burial. A Christian burial. Mrs. Kotz stumbled, and then the poor soul hit her head against a tree."

"No, Pastor. Besides, there's no time. These savages have given us trouble for weeks, especially during the last few days. If I don't get back to them right away, they might make off with the canoe and our supply of flour. There's little enough of that as it is."

"Then you'll have to trust me, Sergeant. I will collect stones and heap them over the body. After that, with her daughter, I will give Mrs. Kotz a Christian burial."

Reverend Burns took his Bible out of his pocket. "You will have to make camp soon. I swear on this Book that I will bring Mrs. Kotz's daughter to your camp before sunset. Are you a Christian, Sergeant Russell?''

The young man stared at the minister for a moment. His face was as impassive as those of the Indians. ''My beliefs are my own affair, Pastor,'' he said. Then he went on. ''But, since we do have to stop before long, I will allow you to go ahead with this burial. Take the daughter with you. If she doesn't quiet down, the savages will do the same for her. Talk to her about that.'' He came back to the river. ''You come with me, ma'am,'' he said to Bertie.

''One more thing, Sergeant Russell,'' Reverend Burns said, in a firm, authorative tone. ''There must be no more threats of scalping. Tell the savages that. There are things you must not expect us to have to bear. After all, you and I — and this poor woman — are civilized human beings.''

''You forget, Pastor, as white men we are disrupting another kind of civilization here in these hills. We are aggressors, too. I agree with you, though. There will be no talk of this death in the camp or in the canoe. I will tell the Indian once more that the British are not paying ransom for scalps this year. If he wants to display his prizes from the fort to his people when he gets home, he will have to hide them away until then.''

He turned to Bertie. ''Come along then, ma'am. You with that baby. You're lucky your

110

hair is not red, so the Indians will have less interest in kidnapping you and adopting you and a red-haired baby. Besides, the braves with us seem to think you are under the protection of that pastor.''

Bertie picked up her bundle and followed Sergeant Russell. Adelheit was restless. Bertie patted the baby and held her tiny face close to her own. But her mind was in a jumble. Threading through the horror of the last hour rose Sergeant Russell's remark about the validity of an Indian's point of view. And then she recalled Anton's critical comments about the way settlers and trappers were disrupting lives of local Indians, and destroying their holy places. Possibly Anton and Sergeant Russell, both soldiers, understood why Indian braves — as though ordered to do it by requirements of their culture — stolidly killed anyone who threatened them . . . or who annoyed them.

But I'm not strong enough yet to have much sympathy for somebody who can do what that Indian almost did to Mrs. Kotz, Bertie thought. *I fear I'm going to need all of my strength just to keep my sanity.*

CHAPTER 19

STORMS IN THE NIGHT had cleared the air, and a hot afternoon sun had begun to dry patches of grass along the riverbank.

Bertie and Bridget sat together on a fallen tree limb, apart from the others, and nursed their babies. A dying fire an Indian had started cast a warm glow over weary, frightened faces nearby.

"Bertie," Bridget whispered, "something's gone wrong with me. I fear I have little nourishment for my Patrick."

When she saw Bridget's questioning look she went on, "I christened my baby myself with river water after I saw what happened to poor Mrs. Katz, and I knew for sure we were all in terrible peril. I could wait no longer. My Patrick's hold on life is so slight, I had to assure him a place in Heaven with holy words even if I spoke the words myself."

Bertie found Bridget's religious beliefs confusing, but she wanted to encourage her. I've boiled some water in this cup I borrowed from Sergeant Russell,'' she said. ''See if Patrick will take a few drops.''

When Bridget spoke next it was in a quiet, anxious voice. ''I've been listening along the way to some of the women,'' she said. ''Their words came through a kind of muddle in my mind, but I heard them. Last night must have been like an hour in hell itself for some of them, too. The savages tore children right from the arms of two of those poor souls. One of them cried all afternoon, and the other one just sits and stares.''

Bertie shuddered. ''We are lucky we were inside the storage room when it all began.''

''And now I have come to believe it was only the little Hazen boys the savages wanted from the storage room,'' Bridget went on. ''Possibly the boys are still alive. Savages often adopt our babies and rear them like their own children, you know. One of the older women said that in the savages' hard way of life, few babies grow up, and they like to adopt healthy babies from other tribes. Or even from settlers' families. They sometimes steal the mothers, too, and make slaves of them, but it's really the children they want.''

Bertie found a bit of comfort in knowledge that somewhere in the forest the little Hazen boys might be sleeping in a semblance of safety.

Then she had another comforting thought. "And your mother and brothers, Bridget. They may well be safe, too. Maybe those awful sounds in the courtyard last night meant that children were being stolen, not that people were being — killed."

"There were other sounds though, too," Bridget said sadly. "Sounds my ears will never forget."

Bertie recalled those sounds. Every terrible thud reverberated again inside her head, with a remembered fear that that smash or that thump could be ending Anton's life.

Bertie was silent for a few moments, taking what comfort she could now from the only secure fact in her life, the fact that she must nourish and protect Adelheit. The night air was soft and warm, and a slight breeze helped to keep mosquitoes away. Here and there women moaned or wept quietly. Some of them conversed in low tones while they baked cornmeal cakes in the fire. Even though the Indians had hunted for rabbits and were roasting them over the fires, the captive women had each been given a half cup of corn meal and told it must last for morning, too. Sgt. Russell had a bit of dried venison. He ate by himself, apart even from Reverend Burns, who sat quietly with Mrs. Katz's daughter, reciting passages from the Bible.

"I pray my parents are safe, Bridget," Bertie said. "I'm thankful now they did not want to come with my husband and me to the fort. And then there's your husband, too. Surely the British and their Indians could not have struck at every farm.''

"I've been thinking about that," Bridget said. "Mr. Metzler will be in perfect despair for our welfare when he hears that the fort was taken." She sighed. "Poor man. Poor, poor man."

Bertie wondered whether Bridget had seen that Indian pointing at her earlier in the day and what it meant. Then she tried not to think of it.

Bridget raised her arm and wiped her sleeve across her eyes. She was crying again.

"You must try not to carry on so for your husband, Bridget," Bertie said, "although I know how you feel. You must keep up your strength to nourish your baby."

"It's not for poor Mr. Metzler I am weeping just at present," she said. Then she leaned closer. "Look at my little Patrick. Look closely, Bertie. His sweet face is pinched and most terribly pale. I must find milk for him."

The baby no longer even whimpered. His skin seemed transparent.

Bertie had heard about wet nurses who cared for children whose mothers were ill, or who had died. She asked hesitantly, "Did one of those women over there by the fire lose a baby last night?" How she could ever bring herself to talk to a distraught mother about such personal things she did not know, but she wanted to help Bridget save her baby, and if it meant asking a grieving woman for milk meant for her own dead child, she would do it.

"No," Bridget said. "I already asked them. I have no pride or shyness when it comes to begging for Patrick. But, no. We will get no help from them."

"Oh, Bridget. I fear I don't have enough nourishment for two babies," Bertie said.

Suddenly two Indians stole out of the forest and strode over to the fire where rabbits were roasting. These men were shorter than the Hurons, and their brief bits of clothing were of cloth rather than of skins. Apparently they were from a local tribe. Although the newcomers spoke in a language different from that of the four, they were able to communicate. Apparently they wanted something.

Once again the Indian who had shouted at Sergeant Russell pointed at Bridget. Then they all turned toward her, and the local braves seemed to evaluate her worth. One of them nodded slightly. After a moment or two they all gestured a farewell, and the visitors were gone as swiftly as they had come.

Bertie felt her stomach begin to churn. The gestures had been unmistakable. And who could protect Bridget and her baby through this long, dark night? Who would even care to?

She heard Bridget's sigh. "Bertie," she said, her voice coming in quick, breathless gasps, "that's a solution. I would do anything to save Patrick's life. Anything. Being a servant to an Indian woman who could nourish my baby would be a great price to pay, it is true. But I would gladly do it."

"Don't say such things, Bridget," Bertie cried. "Don't you remember what you said last night about fighting for your life?"

Bridget reached out for Bertie's hand. "During this long day I think I've found out more about being a mother, and taking on the worries of being a mother. If the Indian had pointed at you, what would you have done?"

Bertie recalled stories about white children — and white men and women, too — who had lived for years as captives of Indian tribes. Some had escaped, and some had chosen to continue to remain with Indian groups they had lived with. And what other choice did Bridget have to save her baby?

"I don't know," Bertie finally said. "You're a brave woman, though. That I do know."

The girl's hand tightened on hers. "No, no," she said, her voice thick. "Not brave. Desperate."

Then Bertie heard her murmur, "I only hope the savages want *me*, too."

CHAPTER 20

BERTIE VOWED TO STAY AWAKE. She lay down next to Bridget, with their babies between them. She reached her hand out to touch the girl's shoulder, meaning to keep it there all night long in case she fell asleep and Bertie tried to leave. Exhaustion soon overcame her and she dropped into a deep sleep.

At some time during the night Adelheit awakened her, and she sat up, her mind in a kind of stupor. Slowly she became aware of the world around her. By now the fire was out, but bright starlight revealed dark forms lying close by, all of them quiet in sleep. Sergeant Russell was visible where he had propped himself against the trunk of a tree. Bertie quickly reached her hand toward Bridget.

"It's all right, Bertie," she whispered. "Go

back to sleep." Relieved, Bertie lay down again and gathered her sleeping baby close to her.

It was still very dark when she woke the next time. Immediately she reached over to Bridget. The girl was not there, but the grass where she had been lying was still warm.

Propping herself on her arm, Bertie peered into the black forest. There was no movement anywhere. The night air was strangely quiet, with no bird calls nor even any cries of animals. Then she saw them, a dark form of mother and child silhouetted Madonna-like at the edge of the river. *Can I be dreaming?*

While Bertie watched, completely mesmerized, two dark figures stole out of the forest and approached Bridget. She turned toward them and raised her hand in the greeting Indians use with each other. Then with a slow, deliberate movement Bridget rose from the river bank and walked toward the two braves, hugging her baby close.

Bertie lay back, utterly spent. Tears streaked across her face. *Why didn't I shout at Sergeant Russell?* she thought. *What kept me from trying to save her?* But she knew. *If I had called out, I could have spoiled everything for her,* she told herself, *And possibly even gotten both of them killed.*

Bertie prayed for Bridget's safety, and she prayed for courage of her own, too, to do what might have to be done in the days ahead.

Sergeant Russell's anger at sunrise over the loss of Bridget and her baby made him snap at the captives and roar at the Indians. Several women reacted with more tears and with fear-filled glances into the forest, but the Indians gazed at their English sergeant with calm unconcern.

"No fire today," he shouted. "I'll give all of you fifteen minutes. No more. This river will start to dry up under us any day now, and then you'll all have to walk. How would you like that?"

"Patience, Sergeant," said Reverend Burns. "The women—and their children, too—must have a few more minutes."

"Enough, Pastor," said Sergeant Russell. "Just shepherd your sheep into their canoe. And keep that rifle I gave you handy, too. I don't want those savages from last night kidnapping the two boys we have left and that last baby."

Somehow the sergeant's harsh words did not frighten Bertie this morning. She felt the local Indians had already taken the captives they wanted.

A bite or two of corncake left from the night before made a meagre breakfast for Bertie. But when she went to pick up her shawl, she found Bridget's cake—left over for her breakfast—on a fold where the girl had placed it for her. She ate the crumbly morsel eagerly. Then she drank some water from the river and washed her face.

She looked longingly at bushes of wild berries a little way upstream, but she knew she dared not risk Sergeant Russell's anger.

It took a half hour to get the women and three children into the canoe. Reverend Burns helped Mrs. Kotz's daughter into the place next to Bertie, and then he sat behind them. Again an Indian faced them.

Bertie's brown cotton dress, with its long sleeves and high neckline, already felt hot, and it was wilted with perspiration from yesterday's heat. But she realized that the long sleeves would protect her from the sun, and she expected to use her shawl the way she had the afternoon before to make a shady shelter for Adelheit.

Closing out the presence of glistening dark skin in front of her, the black scarfed woman on her left, and the shimmering water all around, Bertie bent over her baby and hummed softly. The tune that came to her mind was one Anton had often sung to her. Anton's smile swam before her eyes, but his voice was growing faint. She shut her eyes and listened inside her head for Anton's voice, his laughter, his teasing, comforting words that soothed her and never failed to set her world right.

A moment later she drew a deep breath and turned to the woman sitting on her left. Bertie wanted to comfort her and she began with a tentative gesture. Mrs. Kotz's daughter was sitting with her head down and her hands lying

121

limp in her lap. Bertie reached over and took the woman's hand, and then she held it tightly in her own. She did not know what to do next. She did not even know what her companion's name was. People knew her only as "Mrs. Kotz's daughter," the shadow of an elderly, complaining woman.

Bertie peered around the edge of the woman's black head scarf. The face she saw looked surprisingly young, with large black-lashed blue eyes and a sweet, docile expression. The eyes seemed to focus inward, however, possibly on horrors of the day before.

Finally Reverend Burns leaned forward. "Miss Kotz," he said, "I am sure your sacrifice and Mrs. Metzler's will be the last ones of that sort we will have to bear. Sergeant Russell spelled out to the savages exactly what they were depriving themselves of when they resorted to violence with your poor mother, and when they encouraged local savages to kidnap Mrs. Metzler and her baby. There will be ransoms in Detroit only for live settlers. I believe they understand that now."

Miss Kotz slowly raised her head, and then she pushed her scarf back and turned to him.

"Pastor," she said, "I have reached a conclusion, while I have been sitting here with my prayers. What happened was God's will. Mama never would have survived. Maybe not another day." She paused and shifted her body into a little more comfortable position on her bundle of clothing. "I think now Mama was not in her right mind, not for quite a while. Perhaps the last few days were all like a dream for her. Just a terrible dream, that she must be content at last to have over. That's what I'd like to believe."

Neither Bertie nor Rev. Burns spoke, but Bertie was beginning to respond to the woman's innocence and warmth. Miss Kotz, though, now that she had begun, seemed to want to go on talking.

"And now what will I do with myself? I brought Mama from my brother's farm to the fort for safety when rumors of Indian raids came to us. All my life, day after day, I have been always at Mama's beck and call. That was my life." Her voice was beginning to rise. "What now? What will I do in Detroit? I hear only French people live in Detroit. I will be all alone among French people, odd sorts who are strangers to my language and to my ways of worship. Do these Frenchmen in Detroit speak English, Pastor?"

"I can't say, Miss Kotz," he replied. "But you are not alone. We are all companions here together. And we will want to do all we can to comfort the poor women whose children were stolen at the fort. There will be work for you to do. For all of us to do. But you must not raise your voice, my dear Miss Kotz. That sort of thing is not . . . wise."

Miss Kotz closed her eyes and sighed. She did

not look toward the Indians. But her limp fingers closed around Bertie's hand. A moment later she smiled—a sweet, sad smile. "Let me hold your baby," she said. "Surely your arms need a rest."

When Adelheit was sleeping safely on Miss Kotz's lap, Bertie took a deep breath. She could smell the lush, warm grass along the river, grass already hot beneath the rising sun. A promise of supporting friendships buoyed her spirits slightly. Anton and Bridget and her own parents could all very well be safe somewhere. She prayed that they were. It was all she could do.

CHAPTER 21

THE DAYS THAT FOLLOWED brought them down the ever-widening, ever more swiftly flowing Licking River. Heavy spring rains had kept rivers high in Kentucke County, but there were a good many exhausting treks on foot around rapids and along places where their canoe could not navigate. Sergeant Russell urged them on by telling them that they would soon reach the Ohio River, and then make good travel time.

While they were stopping overnight at an Indian settlement at the mouth of the Licking, where it flowed into the Ohio, Reverend Burns developed a fever. Sergeant Russell boiled water for him to drink and sponged his face, while the pastor tossed about on a blanket in a lean-to, his eyes staring and empty.

Bertie and Miss Kotz and the Widow Schiller,

a dark, glum woman, were given a lean-to at the far edge of the village to sleep in. There were two bearskins spread out on the ground, but they were dirty and smelly, so Bertie pushed them away and sat cross-legged at the edge of the lean-to while she fed Adelheit. Bertie was always hungry now, but she was still able to feed Adelheit and she was thankful for that. Outside the shelter a light rain was falling.

The long-awaited Ohio River looked vast and gray in the mist. The next day promised new anxieties. Paddling upstream hour after hour in those wild currents would be sure to tax even the Indians' untiring muscles, and the canoe would be less stable than on the Licking, where a wearying Indian's turn against the current once threw a little boy into the water. He had nearly drowned.

Bertie sought for a small sense of security by evoking a kind of trick that had worked more than once since she had left her home in the Shenandoah Valley. As a child, when she had had to face a new problem or what seemed like a frightening crisis, she would say to herself, "What would Papa do?" or "What would Mama say?" In recent times she had transferred part of the homage she had paid her parents to Anton, drawing from his strength and his kind of imagination. Now Bertie had only her memory of their influence to guide her. And in the back of her mind lurked the growing fear that her loved ones might no longer be alive. While she sat and watched the rain on the river, she made herself admit that fact for the first time.

And she made herself admit another fact, too. Since the fall of the fort she had begun to transfer her need for guidance to Reverend Burns. Even though his religious beliefs were different from her own, his presence as a pastor had given a kind of continuity to her life. Now he was ill, terribly ill. Even if he should recover, the fever would leave him weak and unable to dominate their little group, to help them ward off fear, and even despair.

Bertie knew that for the first time she was going to have to chart her course by herself. Her parents' teaching could give her support, but from now on her decisions would be her own. And her constant prayers would be for guidance.

"Can't you lie down, Mrs. Marx?" The widow Schiller's complaining voice rose out of the darkness behind her. "It makes me nervous to watch you sitting there. You might attract the attention of one of the Indians." She sat up and turned her face toward Bertie. In faint light from the end of a long summer evening, it was just possible to see her dark, sad eyes and her down-turned mouth. "Pah!" she said. "this robe stinks. I think it has bugs in it, too."

Miss Kotz, apparently too tired to worry about the condition of the bearskin, was already asleep, with her head on her bundle of clothing. She was lying on her back. Her mouth was open and she was snoring slightly.

Bertie decided to ignore the Widow Schiller's complaining. "I do wish I could wash out some things," she said. "I'm afraid my baby will develop a rash, the way Bridget's poor little one did."

"Babies!" the Widow snorted. "Just a lot of trouble. Trouble before they come into the world, and then more trouble afterward." She moved closer to Bertie. "Don't you know what Indians do to keep their young from having rashes? They coat their little bodies with bear grease."

Bertie turned to look at the woman. For the first time the Widow seemed to be interested in someone else. "I do wish I could talk to my mother about all of these things, ma'am," she said. "I'm not sure she would want me to use an Indian method, though, to care for Adelheit." Even as she spoke, she remembered she was still relying on what her mother would say, instead of making her own decision. She would have to think about the bear grease.

Bertie had noticed the woman did not use the word "savage" when she talked about Indians, the way everyone else did. "Have you watched Indians take care of babies?" she asked.

The Widow waited for a moment before she spoke. Then she said, still in her complaining tone, "I'm a half-breed myself, Mrs. Marx. Ma was a full-blooded Cherokee. Pa was a trapper, and when she died birthing me, he took me back to his people in Pennsylvania. Then he left." She sighed. "Nobody ever saw Pa again."

"And you married Mr. Schiller in Pennsylvania?" Bertie asked. It was good to have the woman begin to talk, even though her harsh voice grated on one's ear.

The Widow was silent again. She sat hugging her black-clad knees, and she rocked back and forth a little. "Well," she finally said, "you seem to be a sensible sort, not a goody-goody like that one over there. Schiller was my Pa's name. His family tried to care for me, the way grandparents should love their son's child, but I knew. The little brats I grew up with, especially, made my life miserable. And all the Germans around me knew, too. I was a half-breed. And I always will be."

Bertie recalled the way children at school had taunted a little boy whose grandmother, it was rumored, was a slave in eastern Virginia. She could understand why a person might build a false identity as an adult to try to cope with other people's prejudice. Even the Germans and the Scotch-Irish settlers back home had terrible confrontations from time to time, and then their children yelled at each other about superior ways of doing things. How much worse it was for Indians or for descendents of slaves.

"What then shall I call you?" Bertie asked.

"Are you always known as 'the Widow Schiller'?"

The woman laughed, without mirth. "What, indeed!" she said. "When I was sixteen I decided to go back to live with my mother's people. That story is a long one, and filled with a good deal of cruelty, and of hopelessness at the last, too. My mother's village, when I finally found it, was like a foreign country for me." She paused, apparently remembering. "I became a slave there. A slave for my Indian grandmother.

"What should you call me? From now on I will be simply Frau Schiller. Although I learned Indian ways, because I lived among them serving my grandmother for ten years, I know now I want to be more German than Indian. If I live through this ordeal, I will go back to Pennsylvania, and I will thank Pa's father and mother for all they tried to do for me. If I have a home, I suppose my real home is there."

Bertie was silent for a moment. "That's the reason you know how Indian mothers take care of children?"

Frau Schiller leaned her head on her knees. After a while she sat up again and sighed. "Well, I was married, Mrs. Marx," she said, "after the Indian fashion. I thought I had made a final decision. A decision to live as an Indian.

"But . . . when my babies all died . . . ." She paused and then went on, "Most babies of Indian mothers die in these terrible times, while white settlers and trappers hunt their husbands and sons down and destroy their villages.

"I just grew weary, weary of running and of the killings and of my babies all dying. And then my husband was cut down, too. Not by a white man, but by a Shawnee." She paused again. "When I came to the fort I called myself the Widow Schiller because I thought my husband's name sounded too *Indian* for white people to pronounce. And, of course, these titles have no meaning for Indians."

Bertie touched Frau Schiller's boney, claw-like hand. "If we stay together, we can get to Detroit safely," she said. "We must not fight with each other. We need each other."

"All that keeps me going is the memory of my little bedroom in my grossvatter's fine stone house. Its smells and its colors come to me in dreams, Mrs. Marx." She turned her hand and grasped Bertie's hand in her own hard, calloused fingers. "I will try to be civil to those other weeping fools," she said, "but it's my dreams that will keep *me* alive. If anything does."

CHAPTER 22

JUST BEFORE DAWN BERTIE stole out of their
lean-to. She took Adelheit down to the edge of
the great river, quiet and misty now under a cool,
soft breeze. Quickly, without looking back
toward the Indian village, she peeled Adelheit's
sticky clothing off and then she doused it, along
with some of her own clothes, up and down in
the water. After that she sponged the baby, who
was starting to make sounds of protest, and
wrapped her in a clean blanket. She held her
close, and hummed a soothing melody. Inside an
hour July sunshine would dry and bleach everything she had washed and hung on the canoe's
edge.

When Bertie crept back up the bank she could
hear morning sounds coming from inside a teepee
just beyond their lean-to. Soon Seargent Russell

was shouting, "Fifteen minutes! Everybody in the canoe in fifteen minutes!"

This morning the fifteen minutes stretched to an hour. Reverend Burns' fever was gone, but he was in poor condition to travel all day long in a canoe. Bertie walked over to see him while the others were starting toward the canoe. The women's preparations were subdued and fearful. Beyond them Sergeant Russell was standing on the river bank, his rifle in one hand. In his other hand the Englishman held two strings of glass beads, payment to local Indians for the use of their village.

"I've boiled some water, Reverend Burns," Bertie said. "Try to drink a little of it. Sergeant Russell says he will let me keep a jug of water and a cup close by. The jug still smells of whiskey, but I've rinsed it out as well as I could."

The pastor, still in his black suit, lay on a filthy bearskin at the edge of the lean-to. Odors of sweat and of illness struck Bertie's nostrils, and at once Rev. Burns became for her only a poor invalid who needed her.

He turned his head toward her. His eyes, sunk in dark hollows, were lucid this morining, and his skin was pale now above a new growth of heavy beard. Bertie sat beside him and raised his head to her lap. With her free hand she poured a little water and held the cup to his lips.

"Thank you, Mrs. Marx," he whispered.

"While I have been lying here, I have been thinking about our situation."

"Just rest," Bertie said. "Just rest. You can talk later."

"But I must say something while we are alone," he went on hoarsely. "You are the only strong one among us now. This fever, once it starts, comes back to torture its victims. I fear I won't be able to depend on my health again for a long time."

"I am strong," Bertie replied, more to reassure him than to express confidence in herself. "I feel well, but I am awfully hungry. And now you will need good food to help you get well, too. Some one must tell Sergeant Russell he will have to let us get fish from the river, the way the Indians do."

"Since I can no longer carry a rifle to help Sergeant Russell keep the Hurons in line, the whole burden of getting his hostages to Detroit falls on his shoulders. And he's only a boy. An impatient, surly boy. Maybe you can manage him better than I can, Mrs. Marx."

The pastor lifted his head from Bertie's lap and sat up. He rested his elbows on his knees and gazed with dull eyes at the Ohio, where Bertie now saw glints of sunlight dancing.

Bertie adjusted her sleeping baby into a more secure position inside the sling she had fashioned from her shawl, and then she was just getting to her feet when Sergeant Russell called to them.

"Come on, now!" he shouted. "You, Scot! You and your nurse!"

"Spoken like an arrogant Englishman," Reverend Burns said, with a grim smile. He first knelt on hands and knees, and then slowly, with one hand on Bertie's shoulder, rose to his feet.

"Tell the Sergeant I must walk about for a moment, Mrs. Marx," he said. "I will be at the canoe directly." He started off on a zig-zag course toward the forest.

"If that Scot is not here in five minutes, I'll leave him to the savages," Sergeant Russell growled, when she delivered the message.

Bertie climbed into the canoe and settled herself on her bundle of clothing. She strung her washing along the edge next to her.

"Mrs. Marx," Miss Kotz said, "do you think it would be presumptuous of me to offer to . . . to hold the pastor's head for him? Surely he is too weak to sit up for the whole day."

Bertie smiled. "Do ask him," she said. "I believe he would be grateful."

When at last they began their journey, Bertie sat beside Frau Schiller, and the pastor and Miss Kotz were behind them with his head in her lap. Sergeant Russell, as always, squatted in the stern, where he could keep watch. A constant aura of tension and almost palpable terror that had surrounded all of the captives for days seemed to be held at bay temporarily on this sunny morning. Familiarity with their routine,

135

and the fact that their Indians had not threatened them again, helped to dull the women's fears of possible dangers ahead.

Now that Frau Schiller had begun to talk to Bertie, she apparently was anxious to unload her mind. After a few lengthy pieces of information about Indian ways with medicine and herbs and with preparing food, and then a string of complaints about the heat and her own discomfort, she turned to Bertie abruptly and startled her with a remark that sounded like one the mean-tempered "Widow Schiller" of the last few days would have made.

"And that turncoat husband of yours," she said to Bertie, "I suppose he's faring splendidly as a guest of the British on his way to Detroit. Maybe he's even doing the work of our Sergeant Russell for them in another canoe filled with captives."

Bertie gasped and put her hand to her mouth. She could not trust herself to speak.

But Frau Schiller went on, her black eyes sending darts into Bertie's, "More than likely, though, Herr Marx could even be traveling in style by coach, eating and drinking at taverns with British officers."

Bertie turned to see if the others had heard those awful words. The pastor's eyes were closed, and he appeared to be asleep. But Miss Kotz's face showed curiosity rather than anger.

Does everyone believe such lies about Anton? Bertie thought.

"Did anybody see Mr. Marx go off with a British officer?" Miss Kotz asked. "I know of no one who did." Then she looked straight at Bertie for the first time. "I am sorry to have to say these things, Mrs. Marx," she said, "but I heard rumors of the same sort myself. Your husband, who did seem like quite a gentleman in many ways, was a deserter from the mercenary forces. Is that not so?"

Frau Schiller was watching Bertie closely. "I hear Herr Marx has great charm," she said. "I think he must charm the British, too, just the way he charms young ladies."

Bertie closed her eyes and turned away from the others. Words could not express her anger, nor could she bring to mind civil phrases to form an answer. Her heart pounded.

Finally she spoke, with her gaze directed straight ahead at the impassive brown Indian face in front of her. "My husband," she said in a low voice, "was . . . *is* the most honest, trustworthy man I have ever known." She paused, still groping for civility. "Your words, Frau Schiller, and yours too, Miss Kotz, seem terrible to me. Time will prove you wrong. Very, very wrong."

Before either woman could say anything more Reverend Burns stirred slightly, and then he opened his eyes.

"Only God knows why we do things, Mrs. Marx," he murmured. "He determines how we will live and how we will die. What we call time means nothing in God's sight. If your husband is a lost soul, it is not your fault. Pray for him, Mrs. Marx.''

They are all against him, Bertie thought. *And they are all wrong. Even the pastor thinks Anton is not to be trusted.*

Her resolve to unite their little group, a resolve that had seemed so promising only an hour earlier, had faded. The sun began to beat down stronger on the captives, while their paddlers struggled even farther upstream along the edge of the Ohio. Her diatribe spent, Frau Schiller sank into her old posture and ignored the others. The pastor dozed again. After a few moments Miss Kotz leaned forward and patted Bertie's shoulder.

But Bertie could not respond. She pulled a corner of her shawl over her hair and bent her head above her sleeping baby. She must concentrate on only one resolve: She would keep the family safe for Anton. Wherever he was.

CHAPTER 23

BY NIGHTFALL SERGEANT RUSSELL had brought his captives to a river that would take them north. A small Indian trading post there continued to do business with local settlers and also with British soldiers and their Indian friends from the North. This night Bertie and Miss Kotz and Frau Schiller would sleep not far from the post in the luxury of a cabin with a dirt floor covered with hemp mats.

It was hard to watch people come and go with their provisions while each woman formed her half cup of flour into a little cake with river water and then baked it in a fire.

The two small boys outside the cabin next to Bertie were listless. Not once did they shout or run about the way they had at first, even though they had been confined to the canoe all day.

Their trousers and jackets were dirty, and torn from briars and branches they had brushed against during overland treks.

By the time the long afternoon was over Bertie had made a resolution. She had recalled the way Herr Schultz taunted her father, and Anton, too, on the night of the preaching back in the Shennandoah Valley. They had both borne his jibes with good humor.

"It's not my concern when somebody rails at me," Bertie's father once told her. "That is between him and God to work out."

So she had finally resolved that afternoon to assume leadership of the complaining, starving little group, if not for their sake, for her own. Now she took a deep breath and rose from the fire. She began to walk slowly over to the third cabin, where Sergeant Russell sat in the doorway, cross-legged, watching his prisoners and his Indians. He was eating fish a Huron brave had prepared for him. The Reverend Burns leaned on one elbow near the fire in front of the Sergeant, with a half-eaten morsel of cornbread in his hand.

Sergeant Russell saw Bertie coming toward him. "Get back to your cabin, ma'am," he said. Then he raised his voice so his prisoners and Indians could hear. "You know you're not allowed to leave your cabin without permission."

Bertie kept on walking, with Adelheit in her arms. "Back!" he shouted. He pointed to her cabin, but he did not get up, nor did he reach for his rifle. She went on until she was close enough to sink to the ground near him in order to carry on a conversation the others would not be able to hear, but there was ominous tension in the rest of the group behind her. A setting sun cast a warm light over Sergeant Russell's boyish face. She looked at him with curiosity rather than alarm. The sergeant at once became for Bertie only a frightened youth, daring other people to defy him, and she felt sorry for him.

He seemed about to shout at her again when she asked, quietly, "Is the fish good, Sergeant Russell?" Startled, he stared silently at her for a moment, and then he said, "You know my orders. I am a soldier. I am required to follow orders."

"I understand your problem," Bertie said. "But I fear you and your Indians will need to build litters to carry your starving prisoners before long. I hear we have a good deal of walking still. None of us, Sergeant, will be strong enough to walk unless we have meat. Or fish. And berries, Sergeant. There are berries everywhere in the forest."

She paused, realizing that the first crisis had passed. He was listening to her. But she knew she must make another point, even at the risk of having him start to threaten her again.

"I fear if this goes on much longer you will deliver only corpses to your English officers in Detroit," she said quietly. "Aren't the English requiring Indians to bring them *live* bodies this year?''

Sergeant Russell's face reddened. "It's not for you to give me my orders Frau . . . Marx, is it not? Frau Marx. Prisoners who are a bit lean cause less trouble than fat ones. But I don't have time to explain such wisdom to a woman, a woman prisoner at that. I'll have enough work to do, managing this job all by myself, now that the Scot has turned sickly." He laughed. "Even Hessian women and children have shown themselves stronger than a Scot."

Pastor Burns did not turn his head, but he surely heard the insult.

Bertie sensed somehow that the Sergeant might be relatively receptive to her next request—the most important one—now that he had had a chance to shout his problems out for everyone to hear. She knew she must try again.

"Just tonight, Sergeant," she asked, "could we get some fish from the river? We are so close to the river, and you are right here next to us to watch what we do. Please, please let us have fish. Just for once."

Again she chanced going too far. "Do you have small brothers at home in England?" she asked.

"Enough!" he shouted. "Go on. Go on. Catch some fish and eat them. And you," he went on, pointing at Bertie, "after this I want you to stay away from me."

142

All during the long evening the women and children eagerly set their makeshift nets into the teeming waters of early summer, and they caught and baked and ate fish. They even enjoyed berries the boys had gathered under the watchful gaze of their guards.

When it was growing quite dark Bertie took Pastor Burns some fish, but she discovered that Miss Kotz had been there before her, and she was sitting beside him, reciting after him a Presbyterian prayer-after-meals.

With her stomach pleasantly filled, Bertie slept well. In the morning the captives learned that they had spent the night across the trading post from another group of prisoners taken at Fort Liberty. Miss Kotz was the first to spot the others on the bank only a little way upstream. Even Sergeant Russell's blustering and threats could not keep Miss Kotz from shrieking, "Mrs. O'Haire! Oh, Mrs. O'Haire! Do look this way!"

Bertie, who was just going to step into the canoe, saw Bridget's mother turn and stare, and then bless herself.

"Is that you, Mrs. Marx?" she called, "And is my Bridget there with you?" A man in a British uniform grabbed her arm and almost threw her into a canoe that was just getting under way. With Mrs. O'Haire were Bridget's two little brothers, wan and thin, but apparently quite well.

"Bridget is well," Bertie called, "and her baby too."

Apparently groups of prisoners were supposed to be kept separate from each other, because Sergeant Russell made no move to identify himself to the Englishman in charge of the canoe ahead, and that soldier did not stop to meet with the Sergeant. Instead Sergeant Russell ordered his people out of the canoe. They waited for nearly an hour. Then they started off toward the north, after threading their way through busy river traffic in front of the post.

"Why did you tell Mrs. O'Haire her daughter is well?" Frau Schiller asked. She was seated beside Bertie again this morning. "You know that girl and her baby may be long dead by now."

"Is that what Indians do?" Bertie responded. "I believe you would know about Indian ways better than any of the rest of us. I thought Bridget made a wise choice that night. Letting Indians feed her baby was probably the only way she could have saved him."

Frau Schiller stared at Bertie with her sad, dark-rimmed eyes. "You're always right, Mrs. Marx," she said, in a bitter tone. "That's what's so hard to bear about you." She paused. "Maybe your're right about that husband of yours, too. I pray that you are."

That was her only apology to Bertie for her harsh words of the day before, but, coming from Frau Schiller, the apology was enough for Bertie.

CHAPTER 24

FOR TEN DAYS BERTIE and her companions struggled along between rivers in a haze of heat and of increasing exhaustion. One afternoon a sudden violent storm soaked the captives who were caught where there was nowhere for them to find refuge from the driving rain. They had been dragging slowly over flat, dreary plains for miles, with the Hurons carrying the canoe and what was left of their flour. As soon as the storm threatened, Sergeant Russell ordered the Indians to put their flour beneath the turned-over canoe.

When lightning struck a small, isolated tree nearby, the two little boys screamed and cowered close to their mothers, but Bertie welcomed the rain. She placed her tin cup on the ground, and it soon filled.

She let the rain pelt into her upturned face and

stream through her dust-laden hair and her dirty, ragged clothing. When the force of the storm began to pass she even let the warm rain drift across Adelheit's tiny body. Her baby was no longer plump and rosy, and her crying reminded Bertie of the weak, sickly wailing of Bridget's Patrick.

They all headed north again toward what Sergeant Russell had told them was a great lake, where they could ride once more.

That night Bertie stretched out on her shawl near the others, beneath a small grove of trees, and began her ritual of trying to keep mosquitoes away from Adelheit. Soon a welcome, strong breeze rose, and it chased gnats and mosquitoes into sheltering grass and bushes.

But then a whiff of air brought her a tantalizing smell of roasted rabbit, coming from a nearby copse of trees. The Hurons had caught and roasted rabbits for their meal after they built a fire for the captives, so they could bake their small loaves.

Bertie was desperately hungry. Adelheit had discovered her thumb, and it pained Bertie to watch her suck frantically and then begin to mew and complain like a starving kitten.

"Oh, Anton," she moaned, "I'm almost glad you can't see your little fraulein in such a state."

After her nightly prayers Bertie added a request that she knew the pastor would not have approved of. Nor had her own teaching given her ritual prayers for what she wanted now.

She wanted a miracle. Only a miracle, she felt, could save her child. Sergeant Russell absolutely refused to listen to any more of her pleas for food for the captives.

Even if they reached a river the next day, a river that would lead them into the great lake, as Sergeant Russell and the Hurons had caluclated they should, she was not sure Adelheit could survive. Bertie tried again and again to block out what a swollen stomach like hers meant. She had once seen a lamb that had been caught in a thicket and was near starvation when her father found it. The lamb did not survive.

A lop-sided orange moon rose above the copse of trees where the Hurons had made their camp. Everyone in the captive's group apparently was asleep. Miss Kotz snored, and one of the boys cried out in his sleep, but the exhausted prisoners always dropped off as quickly as they could in order to store their energy, or to escape the misery of their daylight hours.

Suddenly a shadow crossed the moon and immediately Bertie became aware of the presence of a large body bending over her. Before her gasp reached her mouth someone covered her face with a large hand. Then she found herself being lifted and carried rapidly into the night away from the other captives. She kicked and struggled, but in her weakness she was no match for the strength of the bare arm that held her tightly against warm, bare flesh.

147

After a dozen strides, the Indian set Bertie down. They had stopped beneath the shadow of a large bush, out of the moonlight. As soon as his hand left her mouth, Bertie started to scream, but she was silenced when he thrust Adelheit into her arms. He shoved her to the ground, to a sitting position, and then he squatted beside her. The teasing smell of meat he had eaten only a little while before overwhelmed her, even in her terror.

Immediately the Huron put something into her hand. The object was warm. It was food. Rabbit. A whole joint of rabbit meat.

Bertie responded the way a starving dog would have. Never had food tasted so good. She ate with ravenous bites.

Bertie was not even aware of the Huron's leaving her to go back to the place where the other captives slept, but when he reappeared he carried her jug and her cup. In the faint light Bertie watched him pour a little water into the cup. He then poured in something from a pouch into the cup, too. He pointed at the cup and then at Adelheit. Curious, but no longer frightened, Bertie lifted the mixture to her lips. It was sweet. The Indian had put sorghum or honey into the water. Here was food for her baby.

Tears ran down Bertie's face while she reached for the Huron's hand. She pressed the lean, calloused fingers between her own hands, and breathed, "Oh, thank you! Thank you!"

A moment later she dipped a bit of cloth into her cup and offered the sweet liquid to Adelheit. The baby at first rejected the strange object thrust between her lips, but once realizing what the cloth held for her, attacked it as eagerly as Bertie had grasped the rabbit meat.

Bertie turned to thank the Indian once more, but he had gone. Instead she said her thanks in a prayer. A grateful prayer for what, in the middle of this night of hunger and loneliness, truly seemed like a miracle.

CHAPTER 25

IN THE MORNING BERTIE looked with curiosity at the Huron who had given her food the night before. She knew which man it was for in the moonlight she had caught a glimpse of the pattern of beads in his headband. Although the Indians talked with each other, sometimes even shouting and laughing together, they remained a remote, forbidding presence for the captives. Sergeant Russell knew a few words of the Hurons' dialect, and they must have understood at least a little English, but they never gave any indication that they were aware of anything people talked about in the canoe.

At first the Indians' impassive faces and stern manner had frightened Bertie and the other prisoners, but now all of the captives were so desperately weary they thought of the braves as just another hostile force, along with the sergeant's bullying and the misery of midsummer heat and storms.

Both Bertie and Adelheit had slept well during the night, though, and Bertie felt better than she had in a long time. She soaked Adelheit's sucking rag in what was left of the sweet liquid in her cup and gave a corner of the cloth to the baby. She worried a little that this strange kind of food might make Adelheit sick, but she had no choice.

Before they began to walk, Bertie rebraided her hair. She had long since lost her combs, and many mornings she did not feel up to doing even the simplest of tasks. But today she ran her fingers through her tangled curls and then plaited them into two thick braids.

A thin screen of clouds kept the July sun at bay this morning. When they started off, Frau Schiler trudged along beside Bertie. Miss Kotz walked next to the pastor, who was carrying one of the boys.

"I can take your baby for a while, Mrs. Marx," Frau Schiller said. "I'm able to help you a little better when I first begin walking than I am later in the day. My life spent with my mother's people should have made me used to hardships like these, but I fear I am turning out to be a poor traveler."

Bertie gave Adelheit to Frau Schiller. She helped the woman adjust the shawl around her neck. "Is it a mark of manhood for a brave to show no emotion, even when people near him are in trouble?'' Bertie asked. ''I've often felt that, as far as the Hurons are concerned, we might as well be cattle or trees. Do Cherokee men act that way, too?''

''For a Cherokee brave, pain and discomfort do not exist,'' Frau Schiller said. ''And they refuse to admit that they are tired. Ever.'' She paused. ''Maybe that is why it's sometimes hard for them to show kindness and happiness, too. I've often thought about that.''

''Weren't your husband and your Cherokee grandmother kind to you?'' Bertie asked. Such a way of life seemed appalling to her.

Frau Schiller smiled. ''I'm afraid I have given you a bad impression of my people,'' she said. ''My husband was often thoughtful. He was kind when my babies died. And my grandmother was kind to me, too, even though she always made me work hard.

''Inside our family, we are pretty much like Hessian families.''

Bertie noted that Frau Schiller still had not found a place in the world of the white settlers. Maybe she never would.

Less than an hour later Sergeant Russell dropped back to walk beside the pastor. He told Reverend Burns that the Indians said the river they had been looking for was just ahead, beyond the flat, wooded area they were crossing. ''You tell the others,'' Bertie heard him say. ''I'll have to keep my eye on the savages while they are soaking the canoe. Everybody can rest at the river until our canoe is ready."

Frau Schiller heard Sergeant Russell, too. She grimaced. "Poor little man," she said. "He's between the devil and the sea. We all despise him, and he can't trust the Hurons. Just see how he has aged during these few weeks!"

Bertie glanced at the sergeant's grim look as he strode past them toward the Indians. It was obvious that the baby face she had first seen in the night three weeks before at Fort Liberty was now changed into that of a seasoned soldier. He would never look youthful again.

After a short rest, there was a welcome chance to gather and gobble down a few grapes that were ripening along the riverbank. While Sergeant Russell was busy with the Indians, the captives settled thankfully into their places in the canoe.

"Sergeant Russell tells me that it's less than twenty miles downstream to the great lake, Mrs. Marx," Reverend Burns said, leaning forward to talk with her, "and then we will be able to travel all the rest of the way to Detroit by water. I believe the worst part of our ordeal is behind us."

"But I wonder whether my baby can survive for several more days," Bertie murmered.

Reverend Burns said nothing to comfort her. Nor did Miss Kotz nor Frau Schiller. There was nothing for them to say.

Bertie looked around at the others seated behind her in the canoe. Every one of them, even the little boys, stared ahead with dull eyes. The beauty of the blossoming summer weeds along the banks, the sparkling, clear water, a fresh breeze coming off the river, all were lost among the captives.

The Huron's gift of food, and the way he had given it to Bertie, helped to lift her own spirits a little, and she felt a new surge of responsibility for the two boys. *Maybe I can get the Huron to feed them, too,* she thought. *But if I tell anyone about what he did for Adelheit and me, I'm afraid I might scare him off. I'm going to need more of his help, though, if Adelheit is to have a chance of seeing her father again.*

All at once Anton's musical voice returned inside Bertie's head. In her terror and loneliness she had lost it. But now, with the prospect of a haven of safety only a few days away, and a faint hope of more help from the Huron, a little of her old cheerfulness crossed her mind's horizon.

"Take care of our little fraulein," Anton was saying to her once more.

She recalled now the Greek myth Anton had recounted when they had sat together on a log during a warm October evening. Orpheus, Anton had told her, lured Euridice back from the land of the dead by singing his beautiful songs.

Truly, Bertie thought, *this has been a death-like time for me, too. And if God is sending*

Anton's voice to me just now to comfort me, I must not give up hope.

Bertie decided that the rest of the myth had little meaning for her. It was the welcome return of Anton's voice that would give her all the strength she would need.

CHAPTER 26

LATE IN THE AFTERNOON Bertie got her first glimpse of the great lake, rising in the distance far to the east. The countryside around their canoe now was swampy, and mosquitoes buzzed and frogs chirruped among the bogs.

Then, just before sunset, their canoe pulled alongside higher ground, where log buildings and teepees spread out beside winding paths in a large settlement. Farther along the shoreline she could see dozens of canoes and a few flatboats drawn up out of the water for the night.

On the still air floated sounds of horses neighing and of dogs barking, mingling with a din of voices that called out in what sounded like words of English and French, and of various Indian languages.

"All out," shouted Sergeant Russell. "One of

the savages will try to find a cabin or a lean-to for you and then build you a fire. The pastor and I will sleep outside your quarters."

He lifted the now very small bag of flour carefully out of the canoe. "All right, you women," she said. "Line up with your cups for your rations."

Bertie wondered if he would try to buy more flour here for the rest of the journey. She hoped it would be in better condition than the last sack he had bought. Every night she and the other women had to spend a few minutes picking weavils out of it. Maybe this time he might give them corn meal instead. It was always coarse, but it was usually a little fresher.

When Bertie's turn came to have her cup filled half full, she paused. She had decided to make a plea for the little boys. But as soon as she began with "Sergeant Russell, I . . ." the Englishman held up her portion.

"You want food?" he asked. "Food or talk? Not both."

There was no alternative. Bertie sighed. "All right, Sergeant Russell." But after her ration was in her cup, she smiled at him.

"You know," she went on, "those two children need help. And only you can help them." Then she slipped away quickly before he could respond.

Looking back, she noted that the boys' mothers received only the usual half cup apiece, and then a little less for each of their children.

Then out of the corner of her eye she saw her friendly Huron standing in the shadow of a bush. Apparently he had been watching her exchange with the sergeant. As soon as she turned toward him, though, he turned, too, and then he walked away.

As night closed in, Bertie felt her usual surge of loneliness. Her fears for herself and for her loved ones always seemed extreme just at this hour. The women around their fire seldom chatted the way they had at the start of their trek. Everyone was in low spirits.

From inside the filthy cabin Bertie could hear snores and occasional cries arising from troubled sleep. She sat with Adelheit just outside the door, shooing mosquitoes away. Reverend Burns slept on a blanket close by, and Sergeant Russell had gone into the village to buy flour. It was good to be alone like this for a few minutes, Bertie thought, to say her evening prayers and to gaze up at the summer night sky. She prayed that Anton would be seeing the same stars, and that her parents and Bridget were still alive to enjoy the beauty of the land they had all come to love, and to, as the Bible said, feed on its riches.

Bertie looked up sadly. The land's riches were all around her, but she was starving. "Another miracle, dear God," she prayed. "For Adelheit's sake, please grant me another miracle."

She must have dozed with Adelheit secure in

the shawl sling. A touch on Bertie's arm awakened her. At the same time a sinewy hand covered her mouth. This time Bertie felt no terror. There was only relief, a relief that was confirmed when moonlight helped her identify the Huron's familiar headband. Adelheit slept on as Bertie rose to greet him.

Tonight he did not carry her, but he took her by the arm and led her for what seemed like a long time toward an area Bertie decided was the far side of the village. They kept to shadowy back pathways. Indians still squatting or sitting cross-legged by their fires took no notice of them as they weaved their way along the rear sides of the dwellings where there were no doorways.

At last the Huron stopped. He put his hand briefly over Bertie's mouth once more. When he took it away, she nodded her head to let him know she understood that she must not speak. He turned and raised a corner of a blanket hung over the entrance to a cabin. Bertie stooped and went inside and the Huron followed.

On a crude wooden table a rag lamp gave off a murky, smokey light. At the table sat a white man, dressed in shapeless cotton clothes. He had a full black beard, and his black hair hung to his shoulders. Sitting near him on a blanket, on the dirt floor, was an Indian woman, wrapped in a shawl. Among the shadows along the wall stood two nearly naked braves, with their arms folded over their chests.

Bertie pushed her hair away from her face, where it had fallen from its braids. Then she smoothed her dirty, wrinkled dress.

"Bon soir, Madame," the white man said. In broken English, he went on. "And so it is milk you need for your infant, yes? My squaw here has more than enough milk. Our babe does not begin to make full use of her mama's resource.

"Will you be so kind as to offer my wife relief? She would be grateful to you."

Bertie gasped. She had only time to see the three-legged stool the man motioned her toward before she collapsed. With one arm around Adelheit, she put her head on the other arm, that she crooked on the table. She began to weep. For a few minutes it seemed to be impossible for her to gain control of herself, but then she felt the Frenchman's fingers stroking her hair. She looked up at him.

"There, there, ma petite," he said. "I understand how you feel. But these red men, they do not show themselves this way before strangers. You will lose their respect. When your Huron came to me, I could see the respect he has for you."

Bertie sat up straight at once. Adelheit was crying her sickly, thin wail that tore at Bertie's heart. Gratefully she untied the baby's sling, and handed her starving infant over into the arms of the Indian mother.

CHAPTER 27

WHILE BERTIE WATCHED, the Indian woman took Adelheit over to a hemp rug in a far corner. Soon the baby's crying was stilled. Bertie turned to the Huron who had been taking in the drama. The expression on his face was softer than any she had ever seen there before, and she impulsively grasped his strong hands in hers, the way she had the first time he had helped her

"Thank you, my friend," she said, looking straight into his face. "And bless you."

A flickering light rose in the Indian's eyes, and then it died. He pulled his hand away and crossed his arms on his chest.

When Bertie turned back to the table, her host was uncovering a large chunk of cornbread and a piece of roasted venison. She did not fall on the food in the same ravenous way she had devoured the rabbit, but she wasted no time getting to it.

"Not too fast, ma petite," the man said. "You will make yourself ill. See how your bones show and how your eyes sink deep into your pretty face. We must try to put a little fat on those bones. Now, would you prefer water, or wine?"

Bertie took a deep breath. "Water, please." She forced herself to pause for a moment and attempt a little conversation. "Does the Huron understand English?" she began. "Did he tell you I am a prisoner, and that I must go north with him and Sergeant Russell and the others tomorrow? The British will pay him and his friends to bring us safely to Detroit. What will happen to us then, I cannot say."

She could stay away from the food no longer. The Frenchman, with an amused smile, watched her eat. While she ate, he talked. "Yes, Madame, the Huron understands," he said. "But do not try to converse with him. It is best that way, with captives and captors. Keep a distance."

"Sergeant Russell surely keeps his distance from us," Bertie said. "At first I tried to have sympathy for him. He has a task that must be hard for such a young man. But he is cruel. We are all starving, and my baby is dying, and Sergeant Russell says only that he must follow orders. He says his orders were to give us each a half cup of flour a day."

The Frenchman poured a cup of wine for himself. "Sergeant Russell is a soldier, Madame. A soldier must follow orders."

Bertie tried to smoothe her straggling hair. For a moment the only sound inside the cabin came from Adelheit's contented responses to comfort and food.

The Frenchman leaned back slightly on his stool, with his hands around one knee. "You may wonder why I am here, in this place, Madame," he said. "An enemy of these English. Well, war is a strange thing. I am a trapper. And, even for the English, business goes on. So for them I am a businessman first and a Frenchman, an enemy, after that.

"I know citizens of these Indian nations well. I have lived among them for many years. The English, who believe the good Lord Himself is English, and anyone *not* English is no better than a dog, do not get on well with these natives. So they all make use of me, the nations of the red men, and the English, too."

"I feel guilty, eating this fine food," Bertie said, "even though I appreciate what you are doing for me. Back in our cabin, the other captives from our canoe are starving. And some of them have had the fever. There are two little boys, not yet of school age, who must have food. I pray we can all make it to Detroit."

"You are a kind woman, Madame," the man said. "And a strong one. The Huron watched you, and he wanted to help you. There is only so much I can do. We must consider the problems of Sergeant Russell, too. Do you understand his problems, Madame?"

163

Bertie's tone was bitter. "He said he had to keep discipline. And to keep us lean. 'Fat prisoners cause trouble,' he said."

"He is right. To a point. But starving can make rebels, too. It made you a rebel." He paused. "Does your pastor not rebel?"

Even though the Reverend Burns had stood up to Sergeant Russell at first, Bertie realized she had not expected support from him during these last weeks. "The pastor has had the fever," she said. "He has been lucky to survive this ordeal."

"Alors," the Frenchman said, "and so the Huron was right. You are the strong one. And now I have news for you," he went on. "The Huron has heard stories from these Shawnee standing over here in the darkness. The Shawnee tell him a story of a woman and an infant who has hair that is red. The Shawnee tell him you know this woman."

A great lump rose in Bertie's throat. She looked at the Huron and cried, "Oh, they are talking about Bridget and Patrick, aren't they? Can't you speak to me? You must know how much this means to me!"

The Huron stood quietly, with his arms crossed. He said nothing.

"Madame," the Frenchman said, "you must not make demands of your friend in such a way. He does not talk well in English. He says these things to me in his own tongue. Yes, the woman with red hair and her infant are well. The petit garcon grows fat with nourishing from a woman of the Shawnee.''

Bertie could hardly contain her joy. ''Bridget is so smart!'' she said. ''I'm sure some day she will be able to come—''

The Frenchman stopped her. ''Nein, nein, meine frau,'' he said in a firm voice. ''Versthe?''

For a moment Bertie was confused. Probably the Indians could not understand German. Then she knew what mistake she had nearly made, boasting that Bridget would soon escape from the Indians.

''Danke, mein herr,'' she said to the Frenchman.

Then the Huron said something to her host. *I've insulted the Indian,* Bertie thought. *How stupid of me.* But apparently the Huron only meant to let the Frenchman know it was time to take Bertie back.

Her host came around the table to her. The Indian woman was at his side immediately, with Adelheit sleeping in her arms. Bertie placed the sling around her own neck again, and then she grasped the woman's hand. The Frenchman put an arm around his ''femme,'' and then took Bertie's hand. Both of them smiled at her through the murky light.

''Au revoir, ma petite,'' the man said. ''You will soon be safe in Detroit. And then you will see that fine husband of yours that you have talked to the others about. The Huron tells me that some of the walking groups from captured forts and stations have long since reached Detroit.''

Bertie could hardly believe what she had heard. "You have news of my husband? Oh, why didn't you tell me that as soon as I came in your door?"

"No, Madame," he said. "I have no real news. From the Huron is word only that some captives have reached Detroit. I fear I may have raised hopes in your heart. I regret my words, Madame."

He had raised her hopes, Bertie thought. And she was not sorry. She smiled at the two of them and at the Huron, who was standing by the door with the blanket pulled back for her. "You have done everything for me, my friends, that anyone could do," she said. "I thank you all so very much."

"One more thing, Madame," the Frenchman said. "You must not breathe a word of this to anyone. And not any part of this little meeting of ours, either. And do not be so unkind to your Sergeant Russell. It was he, you see, who was an accomplice in this venture tonight. But do not even raise one of those pretty eyelids of yours at him. It is hard for the sergeant, such a young man, to keep the discipline. He must keep the appearance of the hard, stern master. Again, au revoir, ma petite. May Le Bon Dieu go with you."

At once the Huron dropped the blanket over the door and took her arm. While she followed him back to her cabin, Bertie's brain was whirling. Sergeant Russell? An accomplice in helping her? That, she decided, would take some thought.

But when they reached her cabin, Bertie decided to stay just outside the door again, to try to sleep a little more. Reverend Burns still slept, and Sergeant Russell had not yet returned.

Now the moon had risen higher, and it cast a pale glow over the quiet village and the marshy ground around it. Bertie's thoughts and prayers, before she dropped off to sleep at last, sang with the news about walking prisoners from places like Fort Liberty who had already reached Detroit.

When she awoke in the morning, next to her elbow she found a reed basket filled with corn loaves, loaves she knew were meant for the captives inside her cabin.

CHAPTER 28

THEIR JOURNEY ALONG the edge of the great lake and up the river that led to Detroit, a journey that had promised the captives a little less misery than their terrible trek so far, turned out to be just as exhausting.

Bertie noted that the Hurons seemed especially eager to be done with their work for the British. They were ready to start even earlier than usual in the morning, and they were reluctant to pull up to shore at night.

The ground around their first camp was swampy, much like the land around the village had been the night before. But tonight they would have no cabin to sleep in, and the mosquitoes were ravenous. Bertie spread her shawl loosely over Adelheit's face, but her own face and hands were already covered with itching welts.

"The savages can hardly wait to reach their own village near Detroit," Reverend Burns told Bertie, Miss Kotz and Frau Schiller, while they began to prepare their wheat-flour morsel of bread. It was nearly dark, and several of the captives were still recovering from nausea they had suffered all day on the rough waters. Miss Kotz sat by the fire, waiting for her nausea to pass before she began to mix her flour with lake water.

"Why do you call the Hurons 'savages,' Reverend Burns?" Bertie asked. "If they understand what we say, they surely must not like being called such."

The pastor looked at her quietly for a moment. "Of course you are right, Mrs. Marx," he said. "I am convinced these red men can't understand our language, but Christ would not use a term that suggests a human soul is less than human. I suppose I have always used the term the way most people do, because it seems to me that the Indians often do act like savages."

Bertie recalled her conversations with Anton about the way white people had treated the Indians. "Why don't we just call them Hurons?" she suggested.

Reverend Burns answered her in his preaching voice. "For these people 'Huron' would be as wrong as 'savage,' Mrs. Marx. It is a French name. The English word is closer to what they call themselves. Sergeant Russell says *Wyandot* is their own name for their tribe."

"'Wyandot.'" Bertie repeated. "That's a pretty word."

"No matter what they call themselves, I will always remember what one of these savages tried to do to Mama," Miss Kotz said. She started to knead her flour and water. "And I have seen nothing during these last dreadful weeks to change my mind. Even Sergeant Russell, as black-hearted as he is, has some human feeling. I decided he must when he gave us that food this morning. For who else could it have been?" She laughed scornfully. "Surely it was not one of the savages."

Bertie recalled the words of th Frenchman warning her not to say anything about the Indians or about the sergeant. *How I would love to let Miss Kotz know what I know,* she thought, but she realized that before she and Adelheit had been helped, she might have talked the way Miss Kotz did.

The pastor spoke. "I believe, Miss Kotz, we will no longer refer to our captors as savages," he said. "Now that my strength is returning, I am beginning to think about my mission as a pastor again."

Bertie was glad to hear Reverend Burns talking in his old, vigorous way. But even though they were close to the end of their journey, their future, in her eyes, looked clouded.

"I wonder what will happen to us after the British have paid off their bounty to the Indians," she said. "Will we be put into a prison? Surely we won't just be set free, to go back to Kentucke County."

Frau Schiller, who had been quietly nibbling at her meagre supper, looked up at Bertie.

"Of course we will all have to go to prison," she said. "And if your husband, by some miracle, has survived and has been sent to prison at another British fort a long way off, how will you ever find him, Mrs. Marx? And how will your baby survive in a military prison? I am happy that I have only myself to worry about. No husband. No babies. They are all gone. And now I am glad."

"Don't listen to her, my dear Mrs. Marx," Miss Kotz said. "She is so tired and so sick she does not know what she is saying."

Bertie was grateful for Miss Kotz's sympathy, but she knew that Frau Schiller had put Bertie's own fears into words. Somehow it helped her to have the worst finally spoken aloud, rather than bottled up inside her tortured brain.

It rained on the last day. The food that had renewed Bertie's vigor for a few days was only a memory. There were long, ominous silences between Adelheit's spells of crying.

The rain was warm, but Bertie felt a chilly breeze from off the great, gray river. Her cotton dress was torn and threadbare, and her soggy shawl gave her little protection. She glanced at Frau Schiller, grim and silent beside her. With her black hair hanging in wet braids beside her dark face, one would think she was truly an Indian. But she looked more alert, and healthier than either of Bertie's companions. Reverend Burns' beard was dirty, and his sunburned face had new, deep lines. His dark suit hung loosely on his big, thin body. And Miss Kotz's sweet smile no longer grew out of plump cheeks. She looked anxious now, continually worried about yet unknown terrors.

The others sat or lay in small heaps of despondency. Even the boys showed no interest in the palisade that rose out of the mist in the distance on their left—the palisade that was Detroit.

CHAPTER 29

THEIR CANOE DID NOT head for the palisade at
Detroit, but for the far end of what seemed to be
a large, wooded island. It was nearly dark when
the captives, stiff and cold, climbed out of the
canoe. Two men in British uniforms greeted
Sergeant Russell. He stood proud and tall in his
faded and soiled uniform when he saluted, and
then turned back to his prisoners.

"Stay right here," he said. "I will take care of
the savages first. Then I'll find quarters for you."

Bertie watched the braves and soldiers go off
together toward a small shed at the edge of the
forest. There seemed to be little activity here on
this quiet island. A few log buildings and a couple
of teepees stood near the shore, but only a half
dozen small canoes and a flatboat had been
pulled up for the night. The rain had stopped, and

a bright summer sunset clearly displayed the fort far down the mainland on their left.

Adelheit stirred in Bertie's arms, and she leaned over to kiss her baby's forehead. "However will we find your father in this black wilderness, my little fraulein?" she murmured.

In the distance she saw a small group of men next to a log hut. They seemed to be scrutinizing the new arrivals, and talking together about them. But when the men tried to come closer, a soldier stepped out of the building Sergeant Russell had gone into, and he raised his rifle slightly. The men stayed on for a few minutes, but then they turned and walked away.

"They are probably looking for their families," Reverend Burns said. "It must be that none of them belongs to anybody in our group, though. I pray they find their loved ones."

Bertie peered with interest at the men, who were now disappearing into the forest. But if one of those men were Anton, surely he would have come running, in spite of the soldier.

A few minutes later the Indians strode past their group, without glancing their way. They shoved their canoe into the water and began to paddle rapidly around the tip of the island. Then they headed straight toward the mainland. "Their village must be over there," Reverend Burns said.

Sergeant Russell came out of the shed. He waived his arm at the prisoners with a wide, sweeping motion that said, "This way." Bertie picked up her little bag of clothing and followed the pastor and Miss Kotz, who led the group slowly toward the shed. Sergeant Russell looked them over, with a satisfied air. He put his hands on his hips. "Well, we made it," he said. "Come along now to get yourselves properly identified, and then everybody can eat."

There were murmurs of disbelief. Even the little boys only stared with dull eyes at the man they had come to regard as a monster. They all shuffled along behind the sergeant until they came to a narrow, low building.

Inside the first room a man sat at a small table. In front of him were a candle and a large ledger. The candlelight showed his big pock-marked face beneath a dirty white wig. The ruffle on his shirt had brown stains, and his coat was faded. He spoke to them with a weary, careless air. "How do you do, my friends," he said, with a yawn. "Just line up, if you please, and give me the information I need. We will try to get this over with as quickly as possible. But no questions from you. No questions at all. I have no answers for you. Now, then, you with the baby, first of all. And then you women with those boys."

After Bertie had given her name and age, and told him her birthplace and the place in Kentucke County where she had settled, the man motioned her toward a door that led into the next room. He then wrote something beside her name to indicate what would be done with her. Bertie could not read, in the faint light from the candle, exactly what he had written. Could Anton's name have been somewhere in that book, too? Weakly she choked back tears that had begun to fall once again.

Before she left the room she turned to look at the people she had shared so many terrible hours with. Miss Kotz was crying. Bertie knew she was afraid she would be separated from Reverend Burns. All the members of the group looked far different from the German and Scottish families who had sought refuge at Fort Liberty. Their old friends would have recognized none of them now if they had met them on a country road, with their hair hanging in tangled strands, their faces haggard, and their ragged clothing clinging to emaciated bodies.

She turned and stepped inside the next room. There she saw a trestle table with benches on either side. At the fireplace an old man was ladeling hot soup from a big pot into bowls. Then he carried them to the table. Stacks of bread were piled in the center.

"Come, meine frau," the man said, in a voice that was almost a cackle. "Eat. I am a prisoner of these British, too. But we are the survivors."

The food, a watery gruel with beans and chunks of venison floating in it, was food of victory, victory over the darkness that had kept her mind in thrawl during these last days. She carefully spooned a little of the warm liquid into Adelheit's mouth.

The Reverend Burns said a solemn blessing and a prayer of thanksgiving for them before he began to eat. And they all, even Frau Schiller, murmured "Amen."

After eating their soup and bread, the two boys began to get sleepy. Their mothers smoothed their hair back, softly crooning lullabies. Bertie and Miss Kotz joined them in their songs. One of the women whose child had been kidnapped by Indians during the siege of the fort was recovering from a bout with fever, and the food had made her ill. She sat at the table with her head nestled between her arms, crying weakly.

Sergeant Russell opened the door and stepped inside. "Now, my friends," he said, "it wasn't so bad, was it? We are all here. A good many prisoners did not survive the journey. Probably because they did not get such good care as you did. But we survived! My captain commends me for my good work."

Everyone watched the sergeant with hostile eyes. *But did he have to be so hard on us?* Bertie wondered. They had all come to the end of the trek on what, they were convinced, was the verge of starvation.

The sergeant looked about the firelit room. "Well," he said, "I have information for you, too. Tonight you will sleep on pallets in the barracks next door. Tomorrow you will get your assignments. As prisoners, some of you will be sent to the military prison at Detroit, but I believe most of you will be assigned to household work and to farms here on the island. Tomorrow you will know." He grinned at them—a strange, boyish grin in his thin, old-man face. "Until then, sleep well."

Bertie spent a few minutes in front of the fire drying Adelheit's clothing, while the others talked in weary, disjointed sentences. All day long, in the remote corners of her mind, she had rejoiced in the news she had heard about Bridget, even though her own mood had become more and more dismal as the afternoon wore on. Now, while she warmed her skirts and her feet, she was able to think more about Bridget's good fortune. *I must get word to her husband as soon as I can,* Bertie thought.

She chose a pallet just inside the barracks door. It was too dark to see back into the recesses of the room, but the sergeant held a candle for the women to find out where the pallets were before he left, taking the pastor with him. Next to her, Miss Kotz was crying softly. "Things will work out, Miss Kotz," Bertie said, "and then you and Reverend Burns can start on a life together. I'm sure that's what he would like, too. And he will need a companion in his work."

Then Bertie lay down on her pallet, snuggled Adelheit close to her side, and fell asleep before she had finished her prayers.

The sound of someone coming through the door wakened her. She opened one eye slightly. Just outside the door stood a man with a short stub of a candle in his hand. In the upper reaches of the candlelight Bertie saw a blond beard. She summoned all her strength to keep herself from crying out, but her brain told her that a good many men had blond beards, that she very probably was only dreaming, and that a stranger might well mean to harm her or one of the other captives.

But the candle came closer, and then the man holding it lowered it to just a few inches from her face. She kept her eyes closed.

"Dear God," a voice whispered. "Dear God in Heaven. It's you, Bertie. It's really you at last."

With her heart pounding she sat up and flung her arms around the dear, thin body of her husband.

"Oh, Bertie," he said, "I couldn't believe at first that the poor scarecrow who got out of that big canoe tonight was you. I've left the farm where I'm assigned to work, and I've met every canoe for a week. But this time I had to come back to know for sure."

Then Bertie cried, and Adelheit started to wail, too. Anton circled both of them in his arms, while they laughed and cried together.

They woke the other captives with their laughter, and the prisoners all gathered around Bertie's happy family. The stub of Anton's candle melted away into the night.

CHAPTER 30

BUDS ON THE TREES were bursting into fragrant blossoms. Bertie sat on her doorstep with little Johann on her lap. Adelheit, whose blond curls were falling over her blue eyes, jumped up and down the steps, singing a little song in German. Bertie pulled the tiny girl to her side, and then pushed the child's fine hair back and tied it with a green ribbon.

A moment later Bertie and Adelheit saw Anton coming from the field with his hoe on his crippled shoulder, the shoulder that never would really be right again since Anton had been forced to walk hundreds of miles three years before with the prisoners' great cast iron cooking pot over his head. He told jokes about it now, jokes that made Bertie and Adelheit laugh, but it had been months before the skin on his shoulders had healed. When she saw him shift his hoe to a more comfortable position on his shoulder, Bertie recalled her horror when she first heard about what Anton had endured. They had been eating their first meal together at the farm where they had been assigned to work.

"It was you who kept me going, Bertie," he had told her. "I had a lot of time to think while I dragged one foot after another for hundreds of miles, with that cauldron over my head. I thought about what our life together in the years ahead would be like, and I knew we would need to have complete confidence in each other. Even though I hadn't meant to, Bertie, at first I denied you a right our marriage vows gave you. And it wasn't Orpheus and Euridice I thought about, either, but Jacob earning his right to live with Rachel."

He paused, and then he said, "Every day I prayed to be given another chance."

This was a new Anton, Bertie had thought— one she loved more with each new day. "And I think I profited from my ordeal, too." "I learned to trust God to guide me in a way I never would have known if I had stayed safe and secure back there in the Shenandoah Valley. Maybe my prayers were answered, too, in a good many ways."

Anton had hugged her and said, "Amen!"

Now Adelheit ran to meet Anton. The little girl's fair hair shone bright in the sunlight, and she twirled around and around on her way along the path.

"Mama stopped by this morning," Bertie told her husband. "I can always see her coming across the fields. She says she and Papa still feel sad about the death of the old man who lived on this farm, but she's glad the place was vacant just in time for us. She told me, too, that Miss Katz and Reverend Burns got married, and that Bridget Metzler and her husband finally got back the deed to their farm. They're the last ones, I think. And there's more good news. The Indian family Bridget lived with has told the Metzlers they would like to live with them and help work the land and care for the children."

Anton dropped to the step next to her. "Then maybe it's finally over," he said. "Now the Continental Congress has given all of us back the land the British took away. Even when Governor Harrison got us released, and my commander from Hesse sent me my honorable discharge, I had no idea we'd be able to be back here in Kentucke County by planting time."

Anton took his fat little son on his lap and put his arm around Bertie. Immediately Adelheit squeezed herself between her mother and father. Then they all laughed.

Truly it was good, on this fine spring morning, to—as the Psalmist wrote—dwell in the land and feed on its riches.

ABOUT THE AUTHOR

Elaine Watson is an English instructor at Henry Ford Community College in Dearborn, Michigan. She has published numerous articles, and her poetry has appeared in various journals and magazines and in five anthologies. Her books include ANNA'S ROCKING CHAIR (Serenade/Saga) and SCRAPS OF HISTORY, a book of verse. Mrs. Watson and her husband, who teaches history, have three children and three grandchildren.

Mrs. Watson's plot for TO DWELL IN THE LAND grew out of a true account of experiences of a young German couple during the Revolutionary War. The trials of her characters were like those many pioneers had when they came here 'to dwell in this land.'

A Letter To Our Readers

Dear Reader:

In order that we might better contribute to your reading enjoyment, we would appreciate your taking a few minutes to respond to the following questions and return to:

> Editor, Serenade Books
> The Zondervan Publishing House
> 1415 Lake Drive, S.E.
> Grand Rapids, Michigan   49506

1. Did you enjoy reading BEYOND THE SMOKY CURTAIN?

   ☐ Very much. I would like to see more books by this author!
   ☐ Moderately
   ☐ I would have enjoyed it more if _____

2. Where did you purchase this book? _____

3. What influenced your decision to purchase this book?

   ☐ Cover   ☐ Back cover copy
   ☐ Title   ☐ Friends
   ☐ Publicity   ☐ Other _____

4. Would you be interested in reading other Serenade/Serenata or Serenade/Saga Books?

  ☐ Very interested
  ☐ Moderately interested
  ☐ Not interested

5. Please indicate your age range:

  ☐ Under 18   ☐ 25–34   ☐ 46–55
  ☐ 18–24   ☐ 35–45   ☐ Over 55

6. Would you be interested in a Serenade book club? If so, please give us your name and address:

Name _____

Occupation _____

Address _____

City _____ State _____ Zip _____

Serenade Saga books are inspirational romances in historical settings, designed to bring you a joyful, heart-lifting reading experience.

Serenade Saga books available in your local book store:

#1   SUMMER SNOW, Sandy Dengler
#2   CALL HER BLESSED, Jeanette Gilge
#3   INA, Karen Baker Kletzing
#4   JULIANA OF CLOVER HILL,
      Brenda Knight Graham
#5   SONG OF THE NEREIDS, Sandy Dengler
#6   ANNA'S ROCKING CHAIR,
      Elaine Watson
#7   IN LOVE'S OWN TIME,
      Susan C. Feldhake
#8   YANKEE BRIDE, Jane Peart
#9   LIGHT OF MY HEART, Kathleen Karr
#10 LOVE BEYOND SURRENDER,
      Susan C. Feldhake
#11 ALL THE DAYS AFTER SUNDAY,
      Jeannette Gilge
#12 WINTERSPRING, Sandy Dengler
#13 HAND ME DOWN THE DAWN,
      Mary Harwell Sayler
#14 REBEL BRIDE, Jane Peart
#15 SPEAK SOFTLY, LOVE, Kathleen Yapp
#16 FROM THIS DAY FORWARD, Kathleen
      Karr

Serenade Serenata books are inspirational romances in contemporary settings, designed to bring you a joyful, heart-lifting reading experience.

Serenade Serenata books available in your local bookstore:

#1 ON WINGS OF LOVE, Elaine L. Schulte
#2 LOVE'S SWEET PROMISE,
    Susan C. Feldhake
#3 FOR LOVE ALONE, Susan C. Feldhake
#4 LOVE'S LATE SPRING, Lydia Heermann
#5 IN COMES LOVE, Mab Graff Hoover
#6 FOUNTAIN OF LOVE, Velma S. Daniels
    and
    Peggy E. King.
#7 MORNING SONG, Linda Herring
#8 A MOUNTAIN TO STAND STRONG,
    Peggy Darty
#9 LOVE'S PERFECT IMAGE, Judy Baer
#10 SMOKY MOUNTAIN SUNRISE,
    Yvonne Lehman
#11 GREENGOLD AUTUMN,
    Donna Fletcher Crow
#12 IRRESISTIBLE LOVE, Elaine Anne McAvoy
#13 ETERNAL FLAME, Lurlene McDaniel
#14 WINDSONG, Linda Herring
#15 FOREVER EDEN, Barbara Bennett

Watch for other books in both the *Serenade Saga* (historical) and *Serenade Serenata* (contemporary) series coming soon.